C000003092

ABOUT THE AUTHOR

Rick Wood is a British writer born in Cheltenham.

His love for writing came at an early age, as did his battle with mental health. After defeating his demons, he grew up and became a stand-up comedian, then a drama and English teacher, before giving it all up to become a full-time author.

He now lives in Loughborough, where he divides his time between watching horror, reading horror, and writing horror.

ALSO BY RICK WOOD

The Sensitives
The Sensitives
My Exorcism Killed Me
Close to Death
Demon's Daughter
Questions for the Devil
Repent
The Resurgence
Until the End

Blood Splatter Books
Psycho B*tches
Shutter House
This Book is Full of Bodies
Home Invasion
Woman Scorned

HOME INVASION

RICK WOOD

BLOOD SPLATTER PRESS

Rick also publishes thrillers under the pseudonym Ed Grace...

Jay Sullivan

Assassin Down

Kill Them Quickly

The Bars That Hold Me

A Deadly Weapon

© Copyright Rick Wood 2021

Cover design by bloodsplatterpress.com

With thanks to my Advance Reader Team.

No part of this book may be reproduced without express permission from the author.

CHAPTER ONE

Leon's heavy black boots stepped between one open-mouthed corpse to another.

Their eyes stared up at him. Like they had something to say. Like there was one last retort or beg or plea they had left in them, but they were just too dead to let them out.

It was a good day's work – and he hadn't had many of those in his life.

"Happy?" Joanna asked, wiping the blade of her knife on her jeans, leaving a smear of blood across her thigh.

They could worry about leaving DNA, but what would be the point? It was everywhere. So long as they completed their mission, the law could do whatever they wanted with them.

Hell, he'd probably end up in prison whatever he did. He was jobless. On the dole. Without remorse. The kind of person a jury liked to convict.

He looked from Joanna, his girlfriend, to Roman, his faithful accomplice, and to Declan, his older brother.

Oh, Declan… The piece of shit…

Leon didn't care whether Declan had learning disabilities or not – what he'd done was stupid. He'd suddenly developed

1

a conscience in the midst of their attack, and had almost ruined everything.

The kid had almost escaped because of Declan.

Almost.

"If you ever pull that shit again," Leon said, pointing at Declan with his knife, "I will gut you."

"Sorry, Leon."

"We don't have time for shit like that."

"Sorry, Leon."

"I fucking mean it."

"I am sorry, Leon."

Leon let it go. Turned to Roman. Gave him a nod – his way of communicating *well done.* Then he turned to Joanna and shoved his mouth against hers, forcing her into an open-mouthed kiss, both vigorous and aggressive, and she was only too happy to reciprocate.

Then he stepped back. Surveyed the carnage again. Felt a sting of pride. This was the first of two families, and their mission was only half-completed, but it felt like justice had been done.

He looked to the others, raised his fist into the air, and said, "For Jamal."

Each of them followed, raising their fists and echoing, "For Jamal."

His little brother would be proud. Just like the way his little brother had always made Leon proud. Never taking shit from anyone. Punching the bullies at school. Telling the police officers to go fuck themselves.

Jamal's death would always be in vain, and it would never stop hurting, but this family's fate had made him feel a little better.

He turned toward the door. They had to go. They couldn't wait around. The darkness of night would only disguise their escape for so long.

He just couldn't leave.

He had to savour it. He had to look at what they'd done, feel the satisfaction it gave him, glancing from one dead fuck to the other.

The father was the guilty one, and one could say it was unfair to kill his wife and child too – but Leon had no choice. They had to cause this man as much pain as possible, and Leon had achieved that by slowly killing the boy, fucking his wife while she screamed, then slitting her throat just after telling her he would let her go.

The father cried. Oh, how he cried.

The bastard got what he deserved.

"Leon?" Roman said. "Time to go."

Leon nodded.

"Yeah…" he said, looking again at the faces, feeling a little less hurt but no less angry.

"Leon?"

That was Joanna's voice, but he wasn't listening.

He couldn't take his eyes away.

He felt her hand on his arm.

"Leon, come on," she said. "Let's go."

He looked at her. So beautiful. So fucked up. So perfect. TV crews had made crime documentaries about the things she'd done. They'd watched them together, gloating to anyone nearby that she was a star.

"Fine," Leon said, eventually, small and faint.

She pulled him gently toward the door.

He did not take his eyes off the family until he was out of the house and the door was closed.

As soon as they were out, they put their hats on and their hoods up, and were in the car in less than ten seconds. Roman drove while Leon stared in the rear-view mirror until the house was out of sight; until it was like they'd never been there.

CHAPTER TWO

I t's an odd feeling when you leave a job. You spend year after year working hard and forming relationships with colleagues, then it's over, just like that.

Noah was worried he'd regret it. But he didn't. It was the right decision.

He couldn't work for these people anymore.

Maybe he'd do some pro bono work. He could be a lawyer for one of those people who can't usually afford him. Give back to the community what he's taken.

Either way, he couldn't keep defending criminals he knew in his gut to be guilty. He couldn't witness any more victims crying because their killer or rapist or attacker was let free. He'd always stand in the middle of the courtroom, watching them, thinking, *I did that.*

He finished putting his stuff in his box. Despite how long he'd worked here, he didn't have much. A mouse he'd brought in from home, his diary, and his mug.

Eight years and that was all he had to show for it.

He turned to go, and considered saying goodbye to his boss. They'd been good friends, and he knew they'd been considering him for promotion. But he always knew that, should he say goodbye, they would try and get him to stay, and he didn't want to get into another argument.

And so, with a sigh, he turned to go – then stopped as he noticed the new junior associate at his computer, head in hands, shaking his head.

Noah knew how he felt. He'd been this kid not so long ago, tormenting himself with the question of whether he was doing the right thing. It takes a lot of time and self-exploration to discover whether you're the kind of person who can both defend the bad guys, and find a way to sleep at night.

Noah put his box down, went to the kitchen, and made a coffee. He brought it out, placed it on the young man's desk, and gave him a smile.

"Chin up," he said. "You're doing fine."

The fella – Harris or Harry or something like that – smiled wearily at Noah.

Then there was nothing left to do. With a last look back, Noah collected his box and walked through the same corridor he'd entered and left through since the day he started working here. It was lined with offices with glass walls, had a floor that made his shoes squeak, and Philodendron Gloriosums either side of the lift doors; a rare plant that only a firm this successful could afford.

He took the lift to the ground floor, nodded one last time at the doorman, placed his box in the back of his Mercedes, and glanced back once more at the building. He'd assumed he would feel some kind of nostalgia, but he only felt relief.

He drove home with a smile, thinking about all the wonderful things he could do with the rest of his day; things he'd never been able to do before. He could watch a television series on Netflix. He could give Aubrey a break from watching Izzy, their baby. He could even pick up Mikey from school.

He entered his estate and drove past a couple holding

hands, a few mothers laughing as their children played on the playground, and a set of balloons on a fence announcing that it was some kid's tenth birthday… Everything seemed just as it should be.

He parked in the garage and entered the house.

"Hello?" he called out.

No response.

"Aubrey, are you there?"

He walked into the living room, where his wife sat on the edge of the sofa, wearing one of her summer dresses. She was doing something on her phone, but she quickly put it away when he walked in.

"It's done," he announced.

She stood. Forced a smile.

"Really?" she said.

"Yep. No going back now."

He held his arms open and she walked into them, placing her head against his chest.

"Man," he said, "I have to find another job now."

"There's no rush. We're fine for now."

"Maybe I'll start my own firm. Only defend people who aren't guilty."

She pulled back and looked into his eyes. What a stunner she was. Even after turning forty and giving birth to two kids, she was still the kind of woman who made a man's knees go weak.

"But how will you know which people are guilty or not guilty?" she asked.

He shrugged. "I'll ask them."

"What if they lie?"

"I'll do a lie detector test."

"You know they don't work, right?"

"Then I will make them pinky promise."

She lifted an eyebrow. "Oh, Noah. Forever the trustful man."

He leaned in and placed his lips on hers, kissing her gently at first, then growing passionate.

The kiss was abruptly interrupted by the sound of Izzy's wailing.

"I better–" Aubrey said.

"No!" Noah said. "Please, allow me. You just put your feet up."

With another kiss, Noah disappeared up the stairs.

CHAPTER THREE

Aubrey watched Noah rush upstairs, feeling the same twinge of guilt she'd grown used to.

Once his footsteps had stopped, and she could faintly hear his voice singing to Izzy, she took her mobile back out of her pocket and opened her messages.

Please reply to me

SHE CONSIDERED IGNORING IT. Thought about blocking the number.

But he'd just find another way.

He always does.

So she replied.

I can't do this anymore.
Not to my family.

```
I'm sorry.
```

A MINUTE WENT PAST, where she thought he'd got the message. She went to the cabinet, chose a bottle of red wine, and poured her and Noah a glass.

They could toast with it. Celebrate. Raise a glass to the future.

And she could stop lying to him.

Three dots appeared on the phone screen. He was replying.

She took a large gulp of her wine and refilled it.

Noah's voice still gently sang in the distance. He was singing *Come What May.*

It was their song.

Her phone pinged. She opened the messages.

```
But I love you.
You can't leave me.
I won't let you.
```

SHE WANTED TO CRY. To scream. To beg him to understand that it was over. But she'd done that before, hadn't she? After every round of "I can't do this anymore" her protests became a little less believable. No wonder he wasn't taking her seriously.

She'd been honest with him, even if she hadn't been honest with Noah. She'd made it explicit she would never leave her husband. That her family was the most important thing in her life.

Then he'd always reply, "In that case, why are you here?"

And she wouldn't have an answer.

Noah stopped singing. His footsteps travelled across the upstairs landing.

She quickly replied:

```
Noah's home.
Don't text me.
```

THEN SHE MUTED his number so the notifications wouldn't appear on her phone, and put it back in her pocket just as Noah appeared in the doorway.

"She's back asleep," he said, then saw the wine. "Oh, that for me?"

"I thought we should do a toast."

"How lovely."

He took his wine, lifted it, then gazed at her expectantly.

"To you," she eventually said. "And your big achievement. I'm proud of you."

"And to you, for supporting me," he said. "Not many wives would agree to their husband quitting their job with nothing else to fall back on. Just more evidence as to how much of an amazing wife you are."

She forced a smile.

They tapped their glasses together.

"And–"

Izzy started crying again. Cutting him off.

"Dammit," he said playfully. "Guess she wants feeding. I'll go get her."

He gave her a quick kiss then rushed back upstairs.

She took the baby's bottle and placed it in the microwave, then checked her messages.

He hadn't replied.

And she couldn't tell whether that was a good or bad thing.

CHAPTER FOUR

L eon's hand was steady as he struck the match and lit the candle.

A photograph of Jamal Louis smiled at Leon from below the candle. His younger brother. Killed by a police officer. Jamal didn't like being manhandled, and the fuzz didn't like Jamal not being cooperative.

He felt Joanna's presence behind him, but she didn't approach. Leon didn't want to be touched. She knew that. It was why their relationship had lasted so long. She knew when to be affectionate, and when to back off.

Declan sat on the armchair in the corner. He wasn't standing in respect of their brother. He didn't understand how these things worked. He was thick as shit. Sometimes Leon wondered whether he should even bother keeping him around.

But he'd already lost one brother, he didn't want to lose another

Besides, idiot or not, Declan had as much right as he did to avenge Jamal's death as Leon.

Jamal had been similar to Declan in a way. He didn't have

the learning disabilities Declan had, and Jamal was not as annoying – but, like when Declan was a kid, Jamal hadn't been good at standing up for himself.

Leon remembered when he was in top year of junior school, and Jamal was two years below him. Leon noticed a couple of kids calling Jamal 'ragboy' because of the holes in his jumper. Ma couldn't afford to replace his uniform every year like some of the kids. Leon marched up to the kids and laid them out with a single punch. Their parents were furious, but Ma refused to punish Leon, and he was proud of her for that – she knew Leon only punched someone when they deserved it.

He'd been pissed off with Jamal, however. Jamal should be fighting his own battles. So, for the next week, Leon took Jamal to outside the local private school and taught him to stand up for himself by starting on the posh kids as they walked home; the swots with perfect blazers and ties and ironed trousers and shirts tucked in.

Jamal soon learnt how to throw a good punch against those kids.

Maybe if Leon hadn't taught him how to fight so well, the police officer wouldn't have felt he needed to kill him.

"I'm sorry," Leon said to Jamal's photo. He went to say something else, but it didn't come out.

Leon felt tears pushing, but he refused to cry.

He was a man.

Men don't cry.

Men kill. They maim. They show their tears by tearing apart their aggressor. They destroy those who wronged them. They tear them apart.

But they never cry.

"I hope I've brought you some peace, brother," he said. "I hope the suffering of that family has helped to ease the pain you suffered."

The evidence against the police officer had been strong.

That's what they'd told him.

They said the jury would surely find him guilty.

They had not expected the defence the pig could afford. They had not anticipated how well Michael Logan and Noah Clark would defend him. Thanks to those lawyers, Jamal's killer walked free. The officer was even considered competent to return to active duty. The judge referred to it as "an unfortunate incident."

Leon wouldn't call it an unfortunate incident. He'd call it an assassination.

"We will avenge you again. We will cause the next family all the pain you were caused. Then we will let you rest."

Leon kissed his fingers and made the symbol of the cross on his chest. He held his arms up as he looked to the sky and prayed.

"Please Lord, give us the strength we need to do your bidding. Allow us the power to avenge my brother's death. Bestow on us the lack of mercy we need to ensure they suffer until the last."

He closed his eyes, trusting that the others were doing the same, and gave his silent prayer.

I will do as you did in the flood. In the cities of the plain. To the Egyptian firstborns in the Passover. To the Canaanites. To the Amalekites. Just as you executed or commanded the death of those who threatened your justice, I hear you commanding me, oh Lord, and I will answer. I promise, I will answer.

He opened his eyes.

The windows were shut and everyone was motionless, yet the candle still flickered. He knew that was Jamal, or God, or both. He knew it was their message, their encouragement. Their trust in him to complete his mission.

He turned. Looked at Joanna. She smiled her sexy, sinister smile. Roman stood across the room, silent in respect. And Declan sat, staring up at him like a cowardly piece of shit. He took a moment to appreciate the support he had. The devotion they gave him. Even the mentally deficient one.

He strode out of Jamal's bedroom, followed by the others. He led them down the stairs, into the living room, and turned the television on.

Roman grabbed a few beers from the fridge. Declan took one of his picture books and started reading. Joanna sat beside Leon, taking hold of his hand.

Leon waited. It was a few minutes until the news started, so he turned to Joanna and pressed his lips against hers, opened his mouth, and rubbed his tongue against hers.

As soon as he heard the chimes of BBC News, he broke away and watched.

"Our headlines today. The bodies of a family found dead in Shropshire home. Defence lawyer Michael Logan, his wife, Sylvia Logan, and son, Kyle Logan, were all found murdered in their family home."

The image changed to that of the home Leon had left that morning, sealed off by police tape, people in forensic suits walking in and out.

Leon grinned.

"It's time," he said. "Let's move now."

"You sure?"

"Yes. We've got another family to visit."

CHAPTER FIVE

N oah held the bottle over Izzy's mouth, wandering around the living room, gently bouncing. He didn't even remember he'd left the television on until a news headline caught his attention.

"Our headlines today. The bodies of a family found dead in Shropshire home. Defence lawyer Michael Logan, his wife, Sylvia Logan, and son, Kyle Logan, were all found murdered in their family home."

Noah stopped jigging. Stopped moving. Stared open-mouthed at the woman on the screen reporting on events.

"Their bodies were found by a twelve-year-old boy, a neighbour they paid to mow their lawn. Upon finding the family, the boy immediately fled the house and his parents called 999."

A picture of Michael and his family filled the screen. Noah recognised the picture. It was the one of them on holiday in Hastings from Michael's mantelpiece.

"At this time, police have not commented, and it is not clear what the motivation for these murders were, nor if there are any known suspects."

An elderly woman appeared onscreen, with text at the bottom of the screen indicating that she was a neighbour.

"They were a lovely family, often involved in the community. I'd see Sylvia taking Kyle to school, and we'd say hello. Michael always came around to offer help when I needed it. A lovely, lovely family. And someone... someone butchered them. That's the only word I can use to describe it – *butchered.*"

"It is hard to know what led someone to murder a family held in such high regard by the community," the news reader concluded. "We cannot underestimate the loss that will be felt as a result."

The news went on to another story. The slaughtered family were given two minutes, then it was replaced by a discussion about some meaningless local election.

But Noah didn't forget it. In fact, he heard nothing else the newsreader said. He stood, staring dumbfounded at the screen, not knowing what to think.

Michael had worked at the firm with Noah. The one Noah just quit. In fact, they had both worked together on the Levi Isaacs case.

Levi was a police officer who'd grappled with a criminal and killed him in the process of arresting him – leaving many people accusing him of prejudice toward Jamal Louis. Everyone had assumed Jamal was homeless, so the media didn't seem to care – the assumption was that Jamal was a criminal. That was, until the media found out he had no criminal record, only a mild drug addiction, and wasn't homeless – his appearance had just led to an assumption on the part of the police. With the way the media was focussing on this story, no one had expected them to win the case, least of all the defence.

Yet they had.

Somehow, they had.

It was their biggest victory, the highlight of their career – but for Noah, the celebrations were muted. Yes, he forced a smile as his boss raised a glass, spoke about what a huge victory it was, and hinted that they may end up becoming partners. But inside, he hated himself. Because he had no doubt that the jury had got it wrong. That Levi was guilty. That Jamal Louis did not see justice.

Ultimately, it was the case that made him leave the firm where he'd spent many years building a career. A career that had put his son through private school. Had given him a nice house. Had given his wife the life she wished for. But it was also a career that forced him to live with more guilt than he felt able to handle.

And now he was the only one left to remind the world of the firm's greatest victory – or the firm's abhorrent morals, depending on how one looked at it.

"What is it?" Aubrey asked, appearing in the doorway.

"I…" Noah wasn't even sure where to start.

"Noah? What's the matter?"

The television suddenly sounded too loud. He muted it and turned to his wife.

"Michael Logan is dead."

"Oh my God," she said. Aubrey was good friends with Sylvia, and they'd often had Michael's family around for dinner. "Is Sylvia okay?"

Noah shook his head. "She's dead too."

"And Kyle?"

Noah said nothing.

"Oh, God…" Aubrey sat down, her hand over her mouth. "How?"

"Murdered. It was just on the news. Their neighbour said they were butchered. That's the word she used – *butchered.*"

"But… who would do that?"

Noah gave a non-committal shrug. "I imagine there's quite a list, considering some of the people he's kept out of prison."

Noah suddenly remembered he had his baby in his arms.

She was looking up at him, confused, so he started to bounce a bit again. He'd read somewhere that babies are experts at reading their parent's body language, and he did not want Izzy to see the sorrow on his face.

"You think it was linked to his job?" Aubrey asked.

"There's no way I could know, but if I had to guess…"

"Jeeze. Well, I'm glad you got out when you did."

Noah nodded. He did feel a little relieved he was out. The last thing he wanted was a victim who hadn't received justice targeting him and his family.

Then he felt guilty for thinking such a thing. And sad. And devastated.

They'd killed his whole family. Why would someone do that?

"I just can't believe it, you know?" he said. "He was my friend."

Aubrey nodded. She went to speak, but evidently couldn't find the words.

Noah noticed the time. "I'm going to pick up Mikey from school."

"Do you want me to take Izzy?"

"It's okay, I'll take her for some fresh air. Give you a break."

They looked at each other for a moment, words going unspoken. He'd never needed her to say that she loved him, he always knew.

"I'm so glad I have you," he said. "I couldn't have left that job without your support. I know we made the right decision."

She smiled, but there was a sadness behind it. Noah assumed it was sadness for Sylvia, Michael and Kyle's death. He had no idea that it was actually guilt. That his words of gratitude had inspired shame. That his adulterous wife had been lying to him, and that she didn't deserve his kind sentiments.

But he was going to find out.

19

CHAPTER SIX

Noah Clark left his house at 14:53, pushing a pram and wearing a dark brown coat. It took him twelve minutes to get to St Matthew's Primary School, where he arrived at 15:05. As he waited, he made a few sounds at his baby, Isabel Clark, and stroked her head a few times. The school bell could be heard at 15:15, and Michael Clark emerged from the school gates at 15:21.

Leon couldn't give a shit about any of that.

This wasn't a military operation. He wasn't concerned with the timings of the day or the whereabouts of Noah's family. What time Noah arrived and how long it took him to get home told Leon nothing about his opponent.

Leon wanted to know about the man himself.

He wanted to know whether Mikey hugged his father when he left the school gates. If the baby cried when she couldn't see her dad. How much Noah spoke to his son, how other parents looked at him, and what his body language was like as he pushed the pram.

He wanted to be as familiar with Noah as he was with himself.

Does he love his family and what is he willing to do for them? Is he a proud man or does he walk with his head hung? Would his wife tell people he's a good person and does she cum when they fuck?

Noah hugged his son, and his son hugged back. Despite being in front of all of his peers, the son was happy to engage in a prolonged hug with his parent. The son's smile was big, which would suggest that Noah picking his son up from school wasn't a common event. Noah spoke to his son and, as he did, he rested a hand on his shoulder and smiled.

Mothers looked at him. He didn't realise, but they were checking him out, charmed by his good looks and how great he was with his kid. Other parents clutched their child's hand, dragging them away as they screamed and moaned; giving Noah one last glance as they left.

Oh, what they'd give to have a husband like him, they'd think, instead of the layabout they have at home.

How little they know about Noah Clark.

He defended murderers. He did his best to help guilty people go free. He sold his soul to whoever paid him the most.

He was not the man all those mothers thought he was. He was not an honourable man; he was a bastard and a liar. If it weren't for him, Levi Isaacs would have ended up in prison. He'd have been bullied by other inmates in the way that filth is when they end up behind bars. He'd be hating every moment, crying himself to sleep, getting a fate worse than death.

Leon wasn't doing this out of a selfish or murderous need – he was doing it out of a sense of moral duty. He was driven by his hatred, yes, but the responsibility was given to him by a god who was happy to smite those who opposed Him.

Noah and Mikey walked home with one of Noah's hands on the pram, and the other interlocked with his son's. His son must be nine or ten. A weird looking kid. Wearing a smart coat and designer shoes, but Leon supposed most of the kids that went to that school wore such clothes. It was a private school after all.

Pah. A private school. Paid for by blood money. Most people who had money had gained it through wickedness. Many of the parents here probably deserved the pain Leon was going to inflict on Noah.

He hated them. Detested them. With a passion.

He remembered being a kid, and asking Ma why Santa brought the other kids an Xbox, but only brought him a DVD. She told him to be grateful for what he had, but those kids had made him feel like shit and he threw a tantrum.

It was only now that he realised how much Ma had to give up to buy him that DVD.

He moved from his position at the end of the street to follow Noah, staying at a distance. He didn't have to stay too far away, mind, as Noah never looked back. He wasn't alert to what was going on around him. He hadn't grown up on the streets, he didn't need to be; he could just pay other people to be alert for him. He was too rich to have to care.

Which was why he hadn't noticed the man who was going to murder him and his family trailing behind him.

CHAPTER SEVEN

"A re you going to pick me up from school every day now?" Mikey asked eagerly.

"Perhaps," Noah replied.

He was enjoying this. It had been years since he'd been home for bedtime, never mind picking his son up from school. It felt good. He actually felt like a father, and began to realise just how much he'd been missing.

He made a decision: he would stop being an absentee father. From now on he was going to savour every moment of his young family growing up. He would be a better father, and a better husband. Mikey would love it, just like when he'd seen Noah at the school gates. Mikey had run up to him and leapt into his arms, without a care for what his peers might say.

"Dad!" he'd said. "You're here! You're picking me up!"

"I sure am."

"That's so cool!"

Noah had received a few glances from mothers, perhaps a bit envious of the adoration he was receiving, but he didn't care. It had been too long since he'd had this.

"And perhaps we can play something later," Noah now said,

pushing the pram with one hand, and Mikey gripping the other.

"You mean like a racing game or something?"

Noah chuckled. "I was thinking more like Scrabble, but we can play something on your Xbox."

"But I just remembered, I don't have any batteries for my second controller."

"We can stop and get some. No problem."

Mikey beamed up at his dad.

They passed another father and son, bickering, the son in the midst of a tantrum and the dad rubbing his sinus.

Noah smiled, a little cockily. He should feel sorry for the other father, tantrums aren't easy to deal with – but he couldn't help feeling smug. It was not something he'd ever had to deal with when it came to Mikey. Aubrey had told him of the odd one when Mikey was younger, but Noah had never witnessed it.

He did wonder if Aubrey resented him sometimes. She'd had to be the full-time mother, at home all day, part of the day's routine; her nags as familiar to Mikey as brushing his teeth or getting dressed. Noah was a novelty. Dad being home happened so little that, when he was, Mikey was desperate to spend time with him. Noah witnessed Mikey being perfect and enthusiastic and keen. Aubrey witnessed the outbursts.

"How come you're here, Dad?" Mikey asked, and Noah sensed a bit of hesitation in his voice; worry that this was just a one-off, and was too good to be true.

"I quit my job today," Noah said.

"Really?"

"Yep."

"Why?"

"Because I didn't like it."

"Why didn't you like it? I thought you did."

Noah stopped. Turned to Mikey. Bent down so they were eye-to-eye.

He didn't want to be the kind of parent who patronised their children, or condescended to them. He wanted to be honest. If they asked a question, he did not wish to fob it off – he wished to answer it.

"I am a criminal defence lawyer; do you know what that means?"

"Kinda."

"It means it's my job to stop people from going to prison, and sometimes that means having to defend bad people. Sometimes it means I stopped people from going to prison when that was where they belonged."

"Why would you do that?"

He bowed his head. Looked around. Tried to figure out how to explain this to an eleven-year-old.

"Because it was my job. And that's why I left it. Because I was not comfortable defending bad people."

"And what are you going to do now?"

Noah smiled. "For now, Mikey, I am going to be a dad. Then I will figure out what to do next. Perhaps I'll defend the good people this time."

"But how can you tell the difference between the good people and the bad people?"

What a question. It was one that Noah struggled to answer.

"Sometimes, you can't. Sometimes they look the same, and you've just got to figure out for yourself whether they are good or bad."

Mikey nodded. He still seemed sad.

"What's the matter?"

"It's just, well – how do I know if I'm a good person?"

Noah grinned. "The fact that you're even asking that means you're a good person. Bad people don't care about such things."

Mikey smiled.

"Come on," Noah said. "Let's go home."

Noah took hold of his son's hand, and the pram, and they continued onwards, completely unaware of how much of their conversation had been overheard, and how much it fuelled the anger of the man walking closely behind.

CHAPTER EIGHT

Noah had barely been home for ten minutes when the doorbell rang. He'd only just settled Mikey in front of the children's television programs and loaded his laptop, ready to research into his next career move, when he was forced from his seat.

He glanced out of the window. It was their neighbour, Verity Cunningham. A local MP, passionate advocate of the community, and someone Noah didn't want to admit he despised. She was the first person to cast judgement on others, but so were most of the people who lived in this neighbourhood – the only difference was that, being a politician, she had the platform to voice her snobbery.

Noah walked to the front door, forced a smile, and opened it.

"Hello Mrs Cunningham," he said. "How can I help?"

"Please, it's Verity," she said, her posh, well-spoken voice full of enthusiasm that always sounded fake, even if it wasn't.

Noah couldn't help staring at a large flap of skin on her neck that shook whenever she moved. She was a short and stout woman, with a face that looked like the illustration of an evil character in a Roald Dahl book. He disliked her because he could never tell what was genuine and what was forced – like any politician, she always spoke with a biased impartiality.

"Hello Verity," Noah corrected. "What can I do for you?"

"Well, I was talking to Aubrey the other day," she answered, with the same tone of voice one would have when reading a book to a three-year-old. "She said that you had left your job, looking for pastures new."

"I have indeed. Last day was today."

"Oh, how lovely! Well, I had my cook make this for you to celebrate."

She thrust forward a large oven dish.

"I did consider wine, as would be customary," she said. "But I am sure you have plenty of wine, so I thought, well, who doesn't like a bit of lasagne?"

"That's very kind of you."

Noah reluctantly took the lasagne from her, and wondered which bin he would scrape it into.

"You put it in for forty minutes on gas mark seven, and not a minute more! Really, my cook, lovely woman, Sandy I think her name is, or possibly Sandra – she makes the most exquisite lasagnes, you are going to adore it."

Not sure what else he could say, Noah repeated, "That's very kind."

"And I'll pop around to collect the dish from you tomorrow."

"No need, really, we'll bring it round once we're done."

"Nonsense! It is no problem. So are you doing anything special to celebrate?"

Noah went to answer, wanting to tell her about the great celebration that Aubrey had planned – but, truth was, this lasagne was more congratulations than Aubrey had given him. She'd been too distracted by her phone to prepare anything special for him.

She hadn't even bought him a card.

She'd bought his sister a card when she passed her driving test. She'd bought the neighbours a card when their son graduated. Hell, she'd bought one for his colleagues she'd never met to congratulate him on moving to a new house.

But she hadn't bought him a card for this.

"So what do you plan to do next?" Verity asked. "Do you have another job lined up, or are you going to be a man of leisure for a while?"

He'd love to pretend that Verity was showing a genuine interest, but he had no doubt she was being nosy so she could gossip about it with other neighbours later.

"I don't quite know yet," Noah said. He was being intentionally elusive, but then again, he wasn't lying. "Perhaps some pro bono work."

"Ah, how charitable of you. Helping out those less fortunate. You are just that kind of man, aren't you, Mr Noah Clark?"

Why on earth had she just used his full name? It sounded so... forced.

"I like to think so." Noah looked back into the living room, where Mikey sat, perfectly content in front of the television without a care in the world. "Oh, I think my son needs me. I'd better go."

"Of course, I don't want to keep you from your family."

"Thank you for the lasagne."

"Oh, it's really no problem. Good luck with it."

He began closing the door.

"Thank you. Good evening."

"Good evening."

Finally, it was closed. He waited until her steps on the gravel grew quieter, then locked the door, and stared at the lasagne.

The cheese sauce ran over the side. It looked uneven and unappetising.

He placed it on the side, just to show Aubrey when she arrived home, hoping they could share a joke or two about it before he threw it all away.

That is, if Aubrey would spend enough time away from her phone to notice.

CHAPTER NINE

Aubrey could not stop looking over her shoulder. It was ridiculous. She hated what she was doing to her family, and she hated Graham for making her do it, but mostly, she hated herself for allowing herself to be seduced.

She'd always believed that a person should take responsibility for their own actions, and that one would not give in to temptation unless there was something in their life that meant they wanted to. But that was the problem – there was nothing wrong with Aubrey's life. Her husband was a decent, honest, caring man, her son was adorable and loyal, and her baby was perfect. She had no idea what had driven her to another man.

She paused outside the door. Pressed the buzzer. Glanced over her shoulder again. That's the problem with lies – they are like snowballs. You drop one, and it rolls down the hill, going faster and faster, gathering more and more lies, until the snowball is too big for you to handle.

It began with one small fib – "I'm staying at a friend's tonight." And now it had become this. An affair with so many lies that even she was struggling to discern what the truth was anymore.

The worst part? The first time she'd lied about where she was going, Noah had smiled and said, "Have a good time," with complete trust. He was happy to look after their children so she could have a night out.

She was a bitch. She had to be. After doing that to him, there was no other way she could describe herself.

"Yes?" Graham's voice said through the intercom.

"It's me."

Graham didn't say anything else. He knew the routine. The unpleasant blast of the buzzer sounded and the lock was released. She opened the door and walked through the graffitied corridors, her steps echoing around the hollow vessel. It was a dump. The guy wasn't even well-off. What had she seen in him?

When she arrived, the door was already open for her, like it had been so many times before. He'd leave it open and wait in the bedroom. This time, however, he was in the kitchen, uncorking a bottle of red wine.

"Would you like a drink?" he said, smiling at her as she entered.

"No thank you."

"Can I take your coat?"

"No, I'm not staying."

"Ah. It's one of those days, is it?"

He poured his glass and leant against the kitchen side, watching her. Dirty plates sat by the sink, an empty bottle of beer perched on top of his Xbox, and his poster of Kelly Brook had ripped a bit more since she was last here.

She was struck, in a way she had refused to realise before, by just how different his life was to hers. He was a bachelor. His flat was so tiny if felt like the walls were closing in on her. He earned very little money. And he was a slob, stood there in pyjamas trousers with his hairy chest on show and his hair unkempt. It was mid-afternoon, but he must have only just gotten out of bed. Did he not even bother to shower anymore?

"I've come to say that it's over," she said.

"Yeah, of course you have. You sound just as sure as you did the last time."

"I can't keep doing this to my family."

Graham shrugged.

"Aren't you even bothered?" she said. "Do you even care that I have a husband, and children?"

"It's not my family."

She turned around to storm out, then changed her mind. She went to throw something, but changed her mind again. She went to shout at Graham, but his grin threw her off.

"I love watching you squirm," he said.

"Fuck you."

"What I want to know," he said, placing his glass on the side and opening the curtain, allowing a little light into his hovel. "Is why you couldn't tell me that by text."

"You weren't listening to my texts."

"Technically, you can't listen to texts, as they are written down."

"I meant–"

"I know what you meant."

Graham picked a pair of knickers off the windowsill. They were red, with frills on the edge. She recognised them immediately.

"You left these here, by the way."

She liked those knickers. She'd bought them to surprise Noah.

"Give them back."

Graham raised his eyebrows.

"I mean it."

"Oh, you mean it?"

"Give them back."

"Come and get them."

She huffed. She didn't want to approach him. This wasn't how it was supposed to go. She was meant to tell him to leave her alone then go.

She took a few steps forward and held out her hand.

"Throw them to me."

"No."

He was still grinning. He was such an arsehole.

"Please."

"Are you begging now?"

With another huff, she charged forward and went to take them from him, but he held them high and out of reach.

"What are we, five?" she said.

"Oh, definitely not. Five-year-olds don't do the things we do."

"Just give them back."

"Give me a kiss and I will."

"Stop being a dick."

"You've heard my terms."

She sighed. Looked around. Gave him a peck on the cheek.

"There," she said.

Graham lowered the pants, and she went to take them, then felt herself scooped up in his arms as he kissed her and her body pressed against his and his lips moved against hers and she tried to resist, but found herself kissing him back.

Eventually, she pulled away. At least, she took her lips away from his; she stayed in his arms.

"Please, Graham. I can't."

"Then go. I'm not making you."

She didn't move.

"I have to go." Her voice was so small.

"Then go."

She still didn't move.

He kissed her again, and this time she didn't even think about resisting.

CHAPTER TEN

O h, Aubrey.

You naughty, naughty girl.

Joanna shook her head in playful disapproval.

Aubrey wasn't even being subtle. Kissing him by the window, in full view of everyone in the street, and in full view of Joanna and her camera phone. She took a few quick shots, not wanting to miss any of the action. But she needn't have worried; the kiss didn't show any sign of ending. So she took a video as well.

Once Aubrey's coat was off and her top was on the floor and her lacey bra had been hastily removed, they finally moved away from the window, finding a sofa or a bed or a bit of floor where they could lie down and commit some sins.

Joanna stopped filming and watched it back.

It was beautiful. The woman who had everything, giving it up for nothing.

She texted it to Leon, knowing he would enjoy it just as much as she did.

What a foolish woman you are.

She'd poisoned men for less. If she was Aubrey's husband,

she would make her regret it. Joanna imagined it would be fairly easy to make Aubrey scream.

Less than half an hour later, Aubrey emerged from the door to the building, her coat back on. She readjusted her hair, then stopped. Leant against the wall with one hand and covered her face with her black glove.

She was the worst. Not only had she knowingly fucked the man, now she was trying to make herself feel bad about it. Like it was something she had to force, like she felt obliged to feel ashamed so she had to convince herself to feel that way. But did she really feel ashamed?

If she did, why did she do it?

She wiped her eyes, but Joanna could see no tears.

Aubrey turned to her reflection in the window of the sandwich shop next door. Checked how she looked.

Guilty, Aubrey. That's how you look. *Guilty.*

Joanna had wondered whether torturing the whole family was fair when it was only the husband who'd committed atrocities against Jamal, but this reaffirmed their mission. This woman deserved everything that was coming to her, and Joanna was going to enjoy watching her die.

Aubrey walked down the street, and Joanna followed, keeping her distance. Aubrey wore heels, but she couldn't walk well in them. Not all women can. Some are like gazelles, balancing with grace, then some are like Aubrey, walking headfirst whilst trying to steady her ankles.

They were *rich woman* heels. Too large to balance a person's weight. Like the bigger the heel was, the more wealth you had to boast about.

Aubrey was stomping home quickly, but not so she could return to her family without them noticing. No, it was so she could have a shower by the time her husband arrived home from picking up their child from school.

Oh, Aubrey.

You silly, silly little rich girl.

Sylvia Logan had been a walkover. A sad sack who lived in the shadow of her husband.

Aubrey was different.

She couldn't live in anyone's shadow. She had to have something for herself, even if she had to go outside of her marriage to find it.

She had a little pride, and plenty of arrogance. She wouldn't beg like Sylvia had – at least, not at first; she'd begin by showing impudence at their audacity for daring to terrorise her family.

Or she'd just look to her husband to do everything for her. To fight the fight. To protect them.

She'd looked at Aubrey's Facebook profile. She was constantly posting quotes from famous feminists. But she was a fraud.

When it came to it, Joanna was sure that Aubrey would tell Leon to leave them alone, then hide behind her husband.

First pride, then the crash – the bigger the ego, the bigger the fall.

And you are going to fall a long way, Aubrey. A *very* long way.

Joanna was sure of it.

And she couldn't wait.

CHAPTER ELEVEN

For Noah, it had been a day of many firsts – picking up his son from school, leaving his job, letting Aubrey have a break from taking care of a crying baby – and, out of all of them, this was his favourite.

Teatime.

Something so small, and so simple, but something that meant so much. He'd missed so many dinners that it felt strange to be sat there, at the head of the table, instead of working late – and it seemed like his family were making an extra effort. Aubrey had come home from her walk and spent ages in the shower, before coming down in a nice dress. Mikey was dressed relatively smartly, for an eleven-year-old at least. Even Izzy was sat peacefully in her baby seat, looking at each of them in turn with eyes of wonder.

There was so much she had yet to learn, and he couldn't wait to be around to teach them to her.

"Verity Cunningham called earlier," Noah said as he filled his and Aubrey's glasses with wine.

"Oh yeah?" Aubrey said, not looking at him. "What did she want?"

"Gave me a lasagne to wish me luck for leaving my job. It's on the side."

Noah waited for her to turn and look at the lasagne, waiting to share a few sniggers. But she didn't look behind her. She didn't even look up.

"So what did you do at school today?" Noah asked Mikey, ignoring his wife's indifference. Being able to talk to Mikey over teatime was something he'd been looking forward to for so long; it was a huge contrast to arriving home late and stressed and kissing the forehead of his sleeping son.

"Not much," Mikey said. "We had police come in."

"Did you?"

"They were giving a talk on knife crime."

"Knife crime? Aren't you a little young for that?"

"They said there's been some knife crime in the area, and they were there to spread awareness."

Noah looked at Aubrey. "Surely not here? I mean, maybe in town, but I don't see us having to deal with it in this kind of area."

"They said that it doesn't matter. It affects all of us."

"I'm not sure about that, but okay, if that's what they say."

It was a little odd. He was paying expensive tuition fees so Noah would get a good education, not learn about yobs stabbing each other in town.

"I don't know how you can talk," Aubrey interjected, "when you have a knife in the cabinet for him to see every day."

"That's not a knife."

"What is it then?"

"It's a ceremonial dagger."

"Is there a difference?"

"There is a huge difference."

Aubrey was talking about the ceremonial dagger he kept in the dining room cabinet. It had a curved blade and a black handle with a symbol on it. The symbol didn't mean much, he only had it because it was a family heirloom. Something his father passed down to Noah, just as his father had passed it down for him.

"Perhaps you'd care to share the difference with our son," Aubrey said.

"Very well." He turned to Mikey. "It is called an athame. Its origin is in magic traditions; wiccans and such. It was even mentioned in a religious text."

"Rubbish!" Aubrey said.

"No, I promise."

"Where?"

"In the Key of Solomon. And that particular knife can in fact be traced back to the Renaissance."

"You are full of nonsense."

Noah winked at his wife. She looked away.

"What else were you–"

Three loud knocks came from the front door.

Noah looked at Aubrey, wondering if she was expecting anyone. Her face was a mixture of confusion and alarm. Who could it even be? Hopefully it wasn't Verity again.

"I'll see who it is," he said, taking his napkin off his lap, wiping his mouth, and leaving the dining room.

He opened the front door.

No one was there.

He peered down the driveway. Around the side of the house.

Nobody.

Probably just some kids.

Then again, it would be unusual to get those kinds of kids in this neighbourhood.

With a shrug, he closed the door and walked back to the dining room. He'd only just sat down when the three knocks sounded again.

He exchanged a look with Aubrey. Whilst his was a look of annoyance, hers was of fear.

"It's okay," he reassured her, then turned to Mikey and said the same thing. "It's okay, I'll see who it is."

He returned to the door. Opened it. The same absence greeted him.

This time, he stepped out of the house. Looked around. It was an expensive street, meaning all the houses were large and quite far apart, and the driveways were big. No one would be able to run to another building in that time without him noticing. They must be hiding somewhere.

"Hello?" he called out.

No one answered.

"Who's there?"

Still, no one answered. Then again, what was he expecting? If someone was trying to piss him off, this would be the way to do it.

"I'm trying to have a nice meal with my family, and you are interrupting that, whoever you are. Leave us alone or I'll be calling the police."

He had one last look around. The bush at the end of his large, neat lawn rustled, but from a small breeze. The flower beds couldn't hide anyone, and the gate at the end of his drive still appeared to be locked.

With a glance over his shoulder, he returned inside, locked the door, and put the latch on.

He walked back into the dining room.

"Who was it?"

He shrugged. "Couldn't tell you."

"Wasn't there anyone there?"

"No, I answered the door and–"

Three loud knocks. Again.

"For Christ's sake," he said, trying not to swear in front of his son.

He charged back through the room, but before he reached the door, a loud crash made him jump. He turned toward the noise. The window smashed.

Noah ran to his son, took him to the ground, and covered his body. Aubrey took Izzy and joined them under the table.

They waited for a moment, listening intently.

Silence screamed throughout the room.

"Wait here," he said and, ignoring Aubrey's objections, he left their hiding place and looked around.

It was a large window, leading to the front lawn, but something had managed to destroy it, leaving shards of glass over the floor.

Among those shards of glass, Noah found the culprit. A brick. No, it was bigger. More like a large rock.

Something was attached to it. A piece of paper fastened via an elastic band.

Noah took the piece of paper and unfolded it. As soon as he saw what it was, his eyes widened and his hands shook and he couldn't move.

It was Michael Logan's obituary, delivered just for him.

CHAPTER TWELVE

The police did all they could. Took statements, checked the property, reassured Noah's family. But he knew how this went. He'd been defending criminals for so long that he knew how much they thrived in this new era of police cuts and lack of resources. A brick through a window wasn't murder, it was just a brick through the window. There wouldn't be checks for DNA or a long investigation; there would just be an acceptance that this 'happens.'

"But what about the obituary?" he asked.

"Probably just someone taunting you. I wouldn't read too much into it."

Noah knew the officer was trying to reassure him. Of course the officer knew it was a potentially dangerous situation, that there could be more to read into it, that this could be seen as a threat, but what could he do? There would be many more people dialling 999 as they stood talking, and another ten or twenty jobs that they had to pick and choose from. If anything, Noah was lucky that they'd actually bothered to show up at all.

As soon as they'd left, he was on the phone to the first

window replacement services he found on Google. He did not wish to leave his house, or his family, exposed to either the elements or perpetrators overnight, so he paid double to the first person who was willing to come out this late.

As the men finished putting the window in place, Noah sat on the sofa, with Izzy sleeping in her bassinet beside him, staring at the obituary.

What was the point? The purpose? The reason why someone would throw this through his window?

Was it a taunt? A threat? A warning?

Or just some delinquent trying to be funny?

Aubrey stepped lightly down the stairs, and walked into the room with her arms wrapped around herself.

"Is he asleep?" Noah asked.

She nodded. "It took him a while, but he's fine."

Noah knew their son would be fine. It was Aubrey he was most worried about.

"And are you okay?" he asked.

"Yeah. Fine."

He stood. Walked toward her with his arms open. "It's okay if you're not."

"I'm fine."

She stepped out of his reach and readjusted the armchair cushions.

"Aubrey?"

Something was wrong. He knew it. And it wasn't just about the brick. There was something else.

"Aubrey?"

She straightened up a few coasters, realigned a few picture frames, moved the remote to beside the television.

"Aubrey, would you stop?"

She wiped a bit of dust off the top of the television.

"Aubrey!"

"What?" she snapped.

"Would you stop it? Would you talk to me?"

"What do you want me to say?"

"Something."

"I just – who could have done this?"

She stopped. Looked at her husband, her arms folded.

"I don't know. A pissed off client, or a bunch of kids. Hell, it may have even been someone at work for all I know."

"What if it isn't? What if it's someone else?"

"Like whom?"

She didn't answer. There looked like there were words poised at her lips, but she wasn't letting them out.

"Like whom, Aubrey?"

She looked away.

"What are you not telling me?"

"I…" She looked like she was about to talk, then, just as he was ready to listen, she waved her arms and walked out of the room saying, "I don't know."

He went to follow her, but was interrupted by one of the workmen.

"We're done," the man said.

Noah looked into the dining room where a brand-new window had been installed. It looked clean.

"Thank you," he said. "Will you invoice me?"

He didn't listen to their answer. He was too busy looking upstairs, where Aubrey had gone, wondering what she was afraid of, who she thought might have done this if it wasn't a disgruntled client.

Once the men had left, Noah saw to Izzy, putting her in her bedroom, hoping she slept through the night, then found Aubrey lying on their bed, her back to the door.

"Aubrey?" he said. "What's going on?"

"Nothing. I mean, can we just…"

"Just what?"

"Can you just… hold me."

Noah smiled. That he could do.

"Of course."

He lay behind her, placed his arm around her, and gave her a kiss on the neck.

"I love you," he said.

"I love you too."

CHAPTER THIRTEEN

I t wasn't that difficult. The door had been left open for the window fixers, with the heating turned up so high that it didn't matter how much cold they let in. Roman had entered the house, dressed like one of the workmen, and Noah hadn't even acknowledged him. He'd passed them, walked upstairs, then up the next set of steps to their loft.

That was where he waited, playing Candy Crush until the dead of night.

3.00 a.m. arrived. He'd waited long enough.

He opened the loft door, slowly and silently, and peered down the stairs. The hallway was dark. Once he was sure it was okay to proceed, he crept down the stairs and paused in the hallway, listening again. He'd done this many times, and frequent pauses were important. Every few steps, he'd pause to listen, checking there were no noises. It was essential he remained unnoticed.

The son didn't have a phone. They'd watched him at school and watched him at home and had never seen one. Sensible parents, not letting a child that age have a phone. Who knew what kind of predators might be lurking online.

He edged past the baby's room, ensuring he did not wake her. That would be the last thing he'd need. No matter how deep parents slept, they were always tuned into their baby's crying, and nothing would get him caught quicker than a wailing baby.

The door to the parent's bedroom was slightly ajar. Roman paused again, peering in, watching the mother and father in bed.

Waiting.

Listening.

He stood there for at least ten minutes, watching them, waiting to see if they'd stir. Noah was snoring quite loudly, meaning he was in the middle of a deep sleep, and Aubrey had ear plugs in to block out the sound.

With one light step after another, Roman entered the bedroom. Noah's phone was on his bedside table, and Aubrey's phone was on hers. He took Noah's first, plugging it into his iPad and installing the required software. Once done, he edged around the bed to Aubrey's and did the same.

He left the room with a glance over his shoulder, smirking at the sleeping couple, thinking, *I'll be seeing you.*

The next task was the landline and router. He couldn't go downstairs, as it was alarmed, but his luck was in; the landline and router were in the upstairs hallway. He cut the wire to both.

With his task finished, he walked back up the steps to the loft. He opened the door, listened, then entered and shut it. He would wait here until morning, until Leon told him that the family had left the house, then he would re-emerge and leave through a bedroom window.

He considered getting some sleep, but he was too excited. He would like to say this had been a difficult task, but it hadn't. He'd destroyed their communication to the outside world and they wouldn't even know.

This family were going to be far easier than the last, and he was going to enjoy watching them suffer.

CHAPTER FOURTEEN

Noah woke up naturally for the first time in years. There was no six o'clock alarm, but his body clock still forced him awake. His first thought was *best get to work*, and he only remembered as he was getting out of bed that he'd quit. It was a pleasant feeling.

He picked up his phone, unlocked it, but did nothing. Again, it was just automatic to pick up his phone and check his emails. But there were no emails anymore.

Aubrey still lay next to him, her eyes closed. She looked so peaceful. So beautiful. He'd often woken up in the dark, and rarely had the opportunity to look at his wife before he left. Now, the light forcing its way through the crack between the curtains was illuminating her beauty, and she looked nothing less than angelic.

He kissed her forehead, went into the ensuite, and had a shower. Without needing to rush, he could just stand beneath the water and let its heat soak his body, the cold of early morning replaced by warmth.

When he returned to the bedroom, drying his hair with a

towel, Aubrey was awake and staring at him. It was odd how you can stand in front of someone, completely naked, and feel no sense of shame or embarrassment whatsoever.

Before she could wish him good morning, he leant over her and kissed her. The kiss grew more passionate, quickly turned into foreplay, and they ended up making love.

He looked her in the eyes as he penetrated her, and she looked back, though she looked a little distant. Her face often looked shocked during sex, but it felt like there was something else. Something bothering her.

Noah told himself it was nonsense, and kissed her as he increased speed, and they came together.

He rested his head on her forehead, and whispered, "I'm going to have to go in the shower again." She laughed. Then he had a thought."Care to join me?"

Once they'd showered together, he dressed, automatically taking out his suit. He'd almost finished buttoning his shirt by the time he realised he didn't need to, and instead put on a t-shirt and jeans.

Mikey was already up, sitting crossed-legged on the living room floor, watching early morning kids' television. There was some cartoon showing people with strangely shaped heads. Kids' programmes were weird nowadays. When he was a kid, his television programs made sense; now kids' TV looks increasingly surreal.

"All right, kiddo?" Noah said, ruffling Mikey's head as he passed him en route to the kitchen.

"Hi, Dad," he said.

He had almost finished making his family's bacon sandwiches when Aubrey came downstairs with Izzy, holding her head against her chest and doing that same bounce he always did when holding the baby.

"How is she?" Noah asked as he approached his wife and daughter.

"Good," Aubrey replied. "Just finished feeding her."

Izzy's eyes locked onto Noah's and he said, with the best baby voice he could produce, "Did you have a nice breakfast? Did you? Did you?"

He had no idea why he repeatedly asked their baby such questions, considering the persistence with which he asked would not prompt a response, but whatever, he was happy. Life was just as a he pictured it.

Once everyone had finished their breakfast, Aubrey took Mikey to school, and he sat with Izzy on his lap, the house feeling suddenly quiet.

Of course, that quiet was shortly broken by Izzy's crying and a nasty odour coming from her nappy.

He took her upstairs, through the hallway, to her bedroom, and placed her on the changing mat.

Then he paused.

He'd just seen something.

He finished Izzy then returned to the hallway, and to the router. The wire was broken. How did that happen?

He kept staring at it. How strange. It looked deliberate, rather than accidental.

Then again, it could have been an accident. Maybe Mikey did it, but didn't want to say anything for fear of Noah being angry. Perhaps he could ask Mikey about it when he got home from school later.

Either way, it was strange.

How could Mikey even have done it?

Noah stared a little longer, then realised that staring wasn't going to do anything, and got on with the rest of his day, dressing Izzy in her warmest clothes and walking out into the cold morning.

He had an important meeting with an old friend from law school about a potential new job, one that could mean something, one where he could defend the good guys. There wasn't as much money in it, but it wasn't about that anymore.

He was so lost in thought about the meeting, hoping it would go well, that he completely forgot about the broken wire.

CHAPTER FIFTEEN

Leon spent lunchtime at a table a few over from Noah, watching him. He handled his baby well, engaged with his friend, and was thoroughly polite with all the waiter staff.

One could almost see him as human.

Leon paid and left. He'd followed Noah for long enough. It was time. He texted the others, instructed them to meet, and waited in the dim light of his council house. Late afternoon arrived and winter brought the dark in. He preferred working in darkness.

Joanna arrived home first, taking off her coat and scarf, giving him a kiss before fetching herself a beer. She offered Leon one, but he said no. He wanted to be focussed.

"Anything new?" he asked as Joanna sat down on the sofa, spreading her legs grandly, taking up as much space as she could.

"Same old. Went to see her fuckboy. Nothing new. Does her husband really not know?"

"Noah is clueless."

"Jesus. He must be blind as fuck. I mean, does he not smell it on her?"

"Perhaps not."

"He's a fucking idiot, ain't he? Got all these degrees and shit, but no idea what his wife is doing all day."

Roman arrived home next, giving Leon a nod and taking the armchair closest to the radiator.

"Anything?" Leon said.

"Nah. Kid was drawing in class. Nothing new."

Leon nodded.

"Well?" Joanna said. "What's the deal? We ready or what?"

Leon stared at her. She was such a special woman. Their love would never be anything like the love between Noah and his adulterous whore. Leon and Joanna's love was explosive and dangerous, not the kind to survive the constraints of marriage; they were liberated without the confines of a social construct.

He stood decisively. Looked from his woman to Roman. Jamal's closest friend from childhood. He was almost as pissed off about what had happened as Leon was.

Almost.

"It's time," Leon said. "We hit them tomorrow night."

Roman nodded approvingly and Joanna pumped her fist into the air, accompanying it with a "yes!"

Joanna had said she was doing this for her loyalty to Leon. Honestly, she was doing it because she was a psycho who loved inflicting torture on others. But it didn't bother Leon. She was good at what she did.

"What about the retard?" Roman asked.

Good point. Declan. He'd almost screwed up what they did at the Logan house because of his filthy conscience. Declan had forgotten what they were doing, and why they were doing it.

This was all the more reason why he needed to come. He needed to learn what people like them did to those who dared cross them.

"Eh, boy!" Leon called upstairs. "Get down here."

Chaotic pounding shook the ceiling. Even Declan's steps were idiotic. He practically stumbled down the stairs, then slowed down and entered the room cautiously.

He stared from one person to the other, his eyes wide like they always were. His movements were stiff and jolted, irregular and bizarre.

"Sit down," Leon said.

The only free chair was a wooden chair in the corner. Declan sat on its edge.

Leon kept a grave, stern face. He needed Declan to understand the situation. Even if the idea of Declan understanding such a simple concept seemed impossible.

He noticed Roman and Joanna grinning. They wanted to laugh at Declan. Leon didn't. They hadn't grown up with him. Roman knew him, sure, but they hadn't lived together. Declan was an idiot, yes, and Leon reminded him of that every day – but if anyone made even a small comment about his brother's learning disabilities, Leon would ensure they regretted it. In fact, when he was younger, Leon was kicked out of school for pounding another student's head with a toilet seat as an act of retaliation for teasing Declan.

The teachers had said he could have killed the kid. He said, in that case, he regretted stopping.

And since their parents had died, it was Leon's job to take care of his two younger brothers. Now he only had one left, he had to ensure Declan was guided correctly.

"We're going to the Clark's house tomorrow night," Leon said. "You understand what that means?"

Declan twitched as he looked at the others, then back to his brother.

"I don't know, Leon."

Leon pounded the wall. "I explained this to you!"

"Sorry, Leon."

"The Clarks are the other family who fucked over Jamal. You remember?"

"I do now, Leon."

"No more fuck-ups this time, yeah?"

"No more fuck-ups, Leon."

"I mean it. You do what I say, you understand?"

"I will, Leon."

He looked to the others.

They looked ready.

"Let's go."

CHAPTER SIXTEEN

Noah met Mikey after school again the next day, and he enjoyed listening to all the things Mikey had done that day – writing a story, his music lessons, when his teacher told him he'd done a good job.

When he arrived home, Aubrey was in the living room with her back to him, too engrossed in something to have noticed the front door opening and closing. Noah took Izzy from her pram and held her as Mikey ran into the kitchen for a snack.

She still didn't react.

"Aubrey?" he said.

She jumped and turned around.

"Oh, God, Noah. You scared me."

She clutched her phone.

"What's the matter?" he asked.

"Nothing."

She quickly locked her phone and put it in her pocket.

Noah stepped toward her and she stepped back.

"What's going on?"

"Nothing. Nothing's going on. I don't know what you mean."

"Which is it?"

"What?"

"Is nothing going on, or do you not know what I mean?"

Mikey rushed in, shovelling mini cheddars into his mouth.

"Mum!" he said, and gave her a hug. "I had the *best* day! I wrote a story about a boy who lost his hat and Mrs Inglewood said I did well and I had a violin lesson and I did really well and then Dad picked me up again!"

She smiled. It was not genuine. He'd seen his wife's smile every day of their lives for sixteen years; he knew when it was forced.

"That's lovely, Mikey," she said.

Mikey gave his mum another hug and planted himself in front of the television, ready to watch CBBC.

Noah continued to stare at Aubrey, confused. He didn't want this discussion to take place in front of their son, but he was worried. There was no kiss to greet him, nor a hug; in fact, there had been no pleasantness at all. Just this hostile coldness, this on edge weariness, this feeling that she was doing something wrong. He trusted Aubrey completely, but the way she was hiding her phone seemed odd.

"Aubrey, I–"

Before Noah could finish whatever he was going to say, Izzy's screams began.

"I'll take her," Aubrey said, rushing over and taking Izzy. "Please can you put the pie in the oven?"

She took their daughter and rushed upstairs. A perfect excuse to escape the situation. An opportunity for her to get her story straight.

Noah stood cluelessly, with nothing but the inane chatter of a children's television program and Izzy's howling shrieks to provide the soundtrack to his confusion. His head throbbed under the pressure.

An hour later, they sat down for tea and Aubrey's cold demeanour remained. She engaged with the children, but said little to him. She did afford him a few glances, but they were brief, just a flicker of eye contact, each one warier than the last.

After tea, Noah played with Mikey on the floor of the living room whilst Aubrey cradled Izzy. After a couple of hours, they put Mikey to bed, and put Izzy to bed, then walked downstairs in silence until they were in the living room, alone.

Noah didn't sit down. Neither did Aubrey. He watched her expectantly, but she just stared at the corner of the room.

"I need to…" Her sentence tailed off as she started walking to the kitchen.

"Aubrey."

"In a minute, I just—"

"Aubrey!" He put an arm across the doorway to stop her. "What is going on?"

"I just need to go sort something out."

"Fine. Sort something out. But first tell me why you've been acting weird since I got home."

"Weird? I'm not acting weird."

"I think I can tell when something is off."

"Noah, I don't know what you mean, I'm not—"

"Stop it, Aubrey. Please, just tell me."

She didn't leave. But she didn't engage either. She looked him in the eyes, like she wanted to say something, like the words were ready to leave her lips, but she would not allow them to escape.

"Fine," Noah said. "You don't want to tell me? Let me show you something."

Her eyes widened. She looked alarmed.

"This way," he said, and led her upstairs.

CHAPTER SEVENTEEN

The darkness concealed Leon's black Ford Fiesta as he marvelled at the way these people lived. He had grown up in a mid-terrace house on a council estate, sharing a room with his two brothers. But the way these people lived... The houses on this street were so big and so far apart that the residents would not even be able to hear their neighbour's screams.

Each house had a large lawn and a long drive concealed from the road by huge, lavish gates. The architecture was modern, but designed to look classic, and the houses no doubt had large back gardens with fancy ornaments, maybe even with swimming pools. The cars he could see between the bars of the gates probably cost more than Leon made in a year.

He felt another jolt of anger. So this was what corruption bought you? This was the luxury one was given for defending a murderer? This was what Levi Isaac's lawyer fees paid for?

He hated them even more.

So long as the rich stayed rich, and the poor stayed poor, the world was as they wanted it.

He shook his head. Thought back to a few years ago. He'd

taken part in a protest against welfare reforms; reforms that meant he and his friends would receive even less benefit money. Ma, should she have still been alive and struggling, would have struggled even more. She already had to choose between her eating dinner, and them having clothes for school. How would she survive if they cut her money further?

But the people in charge didn't care about their protests. The rich politicians said everyone had to take their cuts. This made Leon even more determined to make them listen, but when some guy walked past the protest and called him a scumbag, and he punched them, the next day's headline did not focus on the issue they were protesting about. Instead, they chose to show a picture of him swinging his arm with the headline *Violent Benefit Scroungers*.

He quickly realised that these sycophants would never see him as anything but a piece of dirt, no matter what he did.

"What is it?" Joanna asked from the passenger seat.

"I just… I fucking hate these people."

Joanna grinned. "Then let's enjoy it."

Leon looked over his shoulder. Roman was stone-faced, cold, emotionless. It was his game face, and Leon knew it well.

In the other seat was Declan. Slouched down, his leg bouncing, biting his nails. Nervous as shit.

"You going to be a problem?" Leon asked.

"No, Leon."

"Don't just say no Leon like it's fucking automatic. I mean it. No fuck ups today, yeah?"

"Okay, Leon."

"Say it."

"No fuck ups, Leon."

"Look around. These people are rich because we're not. These people got our brother's killer off then went home to their beautiful houses. Don't that make you fucking sick, Declan? Don't it?"

Declan shifted nervously, and nodded. "Yes, Leon."

Leon peered through the gate. He could just make out Noah in the living room, having a discussion with his wife before going upstairs.

"This is it," he said. "Masks on."

He placed his mask on. It was white, the kind they often wear in theatres. Its mouth was blank and rectangular, the eye slots just big enough for him to see out of. You may think these masks were to disguise their identity. They weren't. Leon couldn't give a fuck if the family saw their faces. They weren't going to survive the night to tell anyone what they looked like.

They were for intimidation.

And they were a statement.

He looked at Joanna, strands of hair falling over her mask.

Roman, who looked scary as fuck.

And Declan, whose mask was skewed. He couldn't even put a fucking mask on right.

Ah well. It'd do.

Leon checked up the street, and down the street. There was no one around.

"Okay," he said, taking out his hunter's knife with the large, curved blade.

Joanna and Roman did the same.

"Let's do this."

They went to get out the car then, just as they did, Leon, added, "Oh, and remember – let's try to have fun, guys. Otherwise, why are we even here?"

CHAPTER EIGHTEEN

Aubrey knew she was being shifty. Knew she was avoiding talking to him, or looking at him, or being alone with him. And she knew he knew. Her façade was cracking. She'd lied for this long but, after another attempt to end things with Graham, here she was again. Helplessly lying.

"Let me show you something," Noah said, and Aubrey felt her eyes widen; what did he have? Was it evidence of her affair? Oh God, what was he about to show her? "This way."

He walked upstairs and she wondered whether she should follow. But what if she didn't? If she just stayed downstairs and refused to come up, wouldn't that make her look even guiltier?

Then again, she couldn't look any guiltier, unless she wrote *I fucked another man* in permanent marker on her forehead.

Reluctantly, she followed him, and he took her to the router in the upstairs hallway.

"See this?" Noah said, crouching down and running his finger down the wire. It had been cut.

"And hang on," he said, noticing something else. He lifted the wire to the landline phone. That had been cut too.

That was all this was? She felt a little relieved, but tried not to show it.

"Did you do this?" he asked.

"What? Why would I do that?"

"I didn't. It was either you or Mikey, and I was inclined to believe it was Mikey, until you started acting shifty."

"But why would I do that?"

Noah stood. Shrugged. "You tell me, Aubrey."

"But I wouldn't–"

"Then tell me why you've been acting so strangely this evening. If this isn't it, then what is it?"

"I– I–"

"Was it a prank? A way to stop me from being able to find a job – after all, how can I look without internet?"

"No!"

"Then why, Aubrey, why are you acting so strangely?"

She glanced at their son's bedroom door.

"Not here," she said.

"Fine," he said, and marched downstairs. She followed and, as soon as they were in the living room, he closed the door.

"What?" he said, getting increasingly irritated. She tried to think of a lie she could tell him, something she'd done that could appease his suspicions that wasn't as bad as an affair.

"Well?" he said again.

"There's nothing to tell."

"You just said not up there. Which implies there is some-thing to tell. Well, we're down here now Aubrey, so what is it?"

"I…"

"For Christ's sake, Aubrey, I'm getting really tired."

She looked around, as if the answers were somewhere in the room.

Then she noticed something.

Outside the window. Movement in the darkness. Figures. Approaching the house.

"What was that?" she said, edging toward the window.

"Oh, don't," he said.

"No, really, I saw something."

"Stop avoiding the subject, you didn't–"

The lights went out. Suddenly, it was so dark she could barely see the outline of his body.

"Noah?" she said.

He said nothing.

She reached out for him and found his hand. She pushed herself against his chest, and his arm went around her, and the anger was replaced by fear.

"Noah?" she said. "What's going on?"

"I don't know, it's probably the trip switch or something. I'll go check–"

Three loud knocks resounded from the front door.

Aubrey quickly looked to Noah's face, wanting to see if he was scared or not, but she couldn't see his features in the darkness.

"Christ's sake," he said, then charged to the front door. She followed, clutching his arm.

"No! Don't go!"

"I'm going to see who it is. I'm fed up of this. The other night and now this!"

"But you don't know who it is."

"It's probably just kids."

"What if it's not?"

"In this neighbourhood? Come on, Aubrey, a brick through the window is one thing, but I doubt there'll be anything more."

"I really don't think we should answer it."

The lights came back on. Noah frowned. Who was doing that?

"See, the lights are back on now," Aubrey insisted. "We can see again."

"There's obviously someone out there messing with something."

"Please, Noah, let's just call the police."

"Call them if you want, but whoever it is, I want to teach them a lesson."

Despite Aubrey's pleading, he opened the door.

CHAPTER NINETEEN

Noah swung the door open, ready to give whoever it was an earful. The tip of a blade pointed at his throat as a masked man charged in, and Noah felt instantly sick.

Noah backed up, keeping his wife behind him.

"What do you want?" he said, his wide eyes fixed on the blade. "Just take what you want."

The man laughed.

"Please, I have money."

"I know you do," came the voice. It was hushed, quiet, menacing.

"You can have whatever, please, just take it."

"I will."

The man forced Noah to back up against the wall.

"Run!" he shouted to Aubrey. "Run!"

The man in the mask tilted his head at her. "What are you waiting for? He told you to run."

Aubrey turned and sprinted through the hallway and the living room.

"Please, just leave my family–"

The man punched Noah's face and his head smacked

against the wall. The man punched it again. Dizziness overcame Noah and he fell to his knees, where he paused, tasting blood dribbling from his nose.

He hoped that Aubrey had made it out, and was calling the police. He had no idea that there was another one of them at the back door. By the time he had been dragged into the living room and shoved onto the floor, so had Aubrey, and they remained on their knees together.

The man who held his weapon against Aubrey's throat looked big. Muscular. His knife arm was rigid and ready. His eyes were wide like an untamed animal.

The man who had spoken, the one Noah already assumed was the leader, removed his mask, revealing the face of a young man with tattoos up his neck and onto his cheek. He couldn't be any older than late teens or early twenties.

"Please," said Noah. "Please, just take what you want and leave."

The man grinned. "I already told you, I plan to."

Noah looked at the stairs, thinking of Mikey and Izzy. He had to make sure these people did not go up those stairs to where his children were.

"My name's Leon," the man said. "And I want to make it clear to you, straight away, that I will know if you're lying to me. And if you lie to me, I hurt you."

The man walked closer, slowly, each step deliberate and sinister.

"Do we understand each other, Noah?" Leon asked, standing over Noah.

How does he know my name?

"Who are you?" Noah asked.

"Oh, we'll get to that," Leon said, and crouched down. "First, I have few questions for you."

"Please…"

"First question. Is there anyone else in the house?"

Noah hesitated, before answering, "No."

Leon smiled and shook his head. "I said not to lie to me, Noah."

He swung his knife so quickly Noah didn't register the movement until it was in his thigh. He cried out in pain, then stifled it, not wanting Mikey to hear. Leon pulled the knife out, and Noah had to stifle his cries again.

"Let's try again, Noah. Is there anyone else in the house?"

He stared at Leon, wincing, blood seeping out of the wound. The pain was sharp and constant.

"I'll be more specific. Is Mikey in the house?"

Noah didn't answer.

Leon held the knife out, ready to stab his leg again.

"Fine," Noah said. "No, he – he's at my mother's. He's having a sleep–"

Leon dug his thumb into the leg wound and Noah stifled another scream.

"The truth."

"Fine, yes, he's in the house!"

Leon took his thumb away.

"And is there anyone else?"

Noah stared at Leon.

"For example, Isabella, your baby daughter?"

"Fine. Yes."

Noah stared at the stairs. It didn't mean he'd let them get to his kids, just because they knew they were there. If Leon even tried to get to the stairs, he'd leap to his feet and tackle him. He didn't care if they'd wounded him, he didn't care how much it hurt; he'd do whatever it took.

"I think we finally understand each other," Leon said. "Next question. Do you know Michael Logan?"

Noah scowled. "Yes."

It slowly dawned on him who had killed Michael Logan, and fear rose through his stomach, and he thought he might

71

throw up. It occurred to him that these were not thieves. They were not after his money or possessions.

They were after *him.*

And they had already shown they were willing to murder.

What was it the woman on the news said about Michael's family? That they had been *butchered*?

"And do you know Levi Isaacs?"

"Yes."

"You defended him, yes?"

"Yes."

"Have you figured out who I am yet?"

Noah looked into his eyes. What did this guy have to do with Levi Isaacs?

Then he realised he'd seen this guy in court. He was Jamal Louis's brother. The criminal Levi killed.

"Please," Noah said, "I left that job. I no longer defend criminals. I didn't think it was right, and I quit, and I'm not like that anymore."

Leon smiled a patronising smile, then stood.

Noah's leg was throbbing, getting even worse from his position knelt on the floor. He looked at Aubrey next to him, seeing her tears trickling down her cheeks. She looked scared in a way he could never have imagined. It was a look that made him want to scream.

But he had to think. He had to be careful. His priority was to keep his children safe.

"My family had nothing to do with this," Noah said. "At least let them go."

The man in the mask behind Aubrey chuckled. Leon shot him a grin.

"My children are innocent. They don't deserve to be hurt."

Noah looked to the stairs.

"Just let them be," he said.

"You really don't want us to go upstairs, do you?" Leon

said. "That's why you keep glancing up there. You don't want us to go up there and find your kids."

"Please, just leave them, and we can settle whatever this is between us."

Leon shook his head with a laugh.

"You're an idiot," he said.

"Please," Noah begged.

"All those fancy degrees and you are still thick as shit," Leon said, then bent over Noah with a condescending grin.

"I'm begging you."

"My friend, you don't get it," Leon said. "There's already someone up there."

Just as he said it, a clatter came from above them.

CHAPTER TWENTY

Joanna reached the top of the drainpipe, pulled the window further open, and climbed into the upstairs hallway. She turned to see Declan struggling to climb in and offered him a hand. She helped him in, and he fell on his arse, creating a large clatter.

"For fuck's sake," Joanna said, closing the window. "Do you want to be any louder?"

She walked through the hallway, gazing at all the framed photos on the wall. Holidays on the beach, wedding day, school photographs with the fancy uniform and the slicked back hair. It painted a picture of a perfect life.

She couldn't wait to pick it apart and destroy it.

The first bedroom she came to had the letters I Z Z Y stuck to the door, with pictures of little monkeys climbing over them. She pushed the door open, letting a little light into a room painted bright pink. She almost gagged. She hated pink.

Beyond a load of stuffed toys and a baby changing station was a cot. In it, a baby, her eyes closed, so peaceful.

"Aw," Joanna said. "How sweet."

She walked in, stood over the cot, and watched the baby's serene slumber, listening to the gentle snores.

Declan, who waited at the doorway, hesitated to come in.

She waved him in. "Come on, knobhead. You know what the plan is. This baby is yours to deal with."

He edged in, reaching the side of the cot, and watched the baby too.

"All yours," she said, patting him on the back and leaving him to it.

She continued through the hallway. Everything looked expensive. Even the frames of the photographs, the random ornaments, the pattern of the wallpaper. They were rich fucks, there was no doubt about it.

Jamal had nothing when he was alive, and he had nothing in death, yet here these people were, living a luxurious life that cost more than she could ever afford. Their mortgage payments alone were probably more than she'd earned in a month at her last cleaning job.

They probably gave to charity, too. These rich fucks often did. It made them feel better about having so much money when they were willing to part with thirty pounds a month to help the less fortunate. As if that made them better people.

She cackled a little.

She was going to enjoy this.

She reached another room, this time with the letters M I K E Y. More monkeys clung to those letters.

She opened the door.

The room was larger than the one she'd shared with her brothers when she was a kid. The night light illuminated a chest of toys in the corner, a desk, a chair shaped like a hand, a Lego trainset, and even more space to walk around in.

"Fucking rich kids," she muttered, and entered.

Mikey was asleep, snoring gently.

She walked through the room, tracing her finger over the edge of his toys, until she reached the chair, where she sat.

The chair rocked. She moved back and forth a little, enjoying the motion. It was quite relaxing actually.

"Hey, Mikey," she said. "Wake up you little shit. I want to talk to you."

CHAPTER TWENTY-ONE

Noah had to do something.
Anything.

They were upstairs doing God-knows-what to his kids, and it was his responsibility to keep them safe.

But how was he meant to protect all of them?

If he ran upstairs, he'd leave his wife alone. If he stayed with his wife, he'd leave his children alone.

He stared up at Leon. Still on his knees. His assailant grinning down at him. With no idea what to do.

Then he remembered – his phone was in his pocket. He pulled it out, put 999 on the screen and showed it to Leon.

"I'll phone the police," he said, hating the quiver he heard in his own voice.

"Will you?" Leon said, all too casually.

The other guy laughed. The one with his knife at Aubrey's throat.

What was so fucking funny?

"You might kill us," Noah said. "But I bet I can put up enough of a fight that you won't manage to kill us all before the police arrive."

"You reckon, huh?"

"I know."

Leon exchanged a smile with the other guy. "Hear that, Roman? He's going to call in the filth."

The other guy took off his mask and dabbed his eyes, tears caused by the laughter. He looked no different to Leon. He was bigger and beefier, but he still had the same grin across his face.

"I mean it," Noah said.

"Go ahead," Leon said, and walked over to the sofa, where he sat back and picked up a copy of *The Guardian*. He flicked through the pages.

Noah looked at Roman, then to Leon, confused.

"You phoning them or what?" Leon asked, not raising his eyes from the newspaper.

Noah looked at his wife. God, she looked terrified. It destroyed him to see her looking like this. He hated it.

Noah pressed dial.

"We're sorry, but you are not able to make this call right now," said the robotic woman's voice down the phone.

Noah glared at his phone, then tried again.

The same message responded.

"Not working?" Leon asked.

What had they done?

"Why don't you try your wife's phone?" Leon insisted. "Go ahead. Roman, get it for him."

Roman put his hand into Aubrey's back pocket, and the thought of his hand brushing her backside made Noah feel sick. She flinched as he pulled the phone out and threw it at Noah's knees.

He lifted the phone, dialled 999, and put it to his ear.

"We're sorry, but you are not able to make this call right now."

Noah dropped the phone.

"I imagine by now you've noticed the router wire cut, and the landline wire cut," Leon said. "Roman disabled all outgoing calls on your mobiles just before he cut that wire. You have no contact to the outside whatsoever."

Leon put the newspaper down, walked across the room, and stopped in front of Noah.

Noah felt pathetic. He was on his knees in his own house, inches from this guy's crotch, staring up at him. He didn't just feel scared, or angry; he felt emasculated. Something only a proud man like Noah could understand.

"Please," he said. "Let us go."

"You may as well stop asking," Leon said. "Because at no point am I going to say, oh, well, seeing as you asked so nicely, we'll all fuck off then. We're here for the night, you get me?"

He bent down until he was inches from Noah's face.

"The *entire* night."

Noah had to fight.

He had no choice.

They might kill him, but they would probably kill him anyway. Just like they did with Michael Logan's family.

They'd slaughtered his entire family.

Reasoning with these people would do nothing.

He thought quickly about how he could do it. He could leap to his feet and rugby tackle Leon. Or he could wrestle the guy – Roman, Leon called him – and at least give Aubrey a chance to run.

"I can see your mind racing," Leon said. "Going over all your options. Thinking about what to do. I bet you're sizing me up right now. And Roman. Aren't you? Thinking about whether you could take us. Thinking about whether you could get his knife. Maybe take me down. Am I right?"

Noah said nothing.

He got ready.

It didn't matter if Leon taunted him. He was going to have to try.

"Just to make sure you don't do anything stupid, I'm going to bring down something we call *leverage.* You're a lawyer, you know what that means, don't you?"

Noah clenched his fist. Took a deep breath.

Here we go.

"Oh, Declan!" Leon called.

Noah froze.

Another one of them walked down the stairs. This one was thinner, and ganglier. His body looked like it was made of thread. His face looked distant, like there was something wrong with him.

He didn't look right.

And he was carrying Izzy in his arms.

"No!" Noah cried.

He went to get up, but Leon stretched his arm and held his knife by his baby's throat.

"You understand what I'll do if you don't back the fuck down, yeah?" he said.

Noah desperately nodded.

"Brilliant."

Leon bent over Noah again, close enough that Noah could feel his assailant's warm breath on his face, so Noah could see Leon's eyes up close.

He tried to find some humanity in them, but all he could see was rage.

"You so much as shift an inch from this spot, and I will cut her throat," Leon told him.

And Noah knew that he meant it.

CHAPTER TWENTY-TWO

M ikey's eyes opened. He could hear talking downstairs. Was it morning already?

He looked at his clock. The small dinosaur's hand was at nine. He hadn't long since come to bed.

So why were they talking so loudly?

He turned. Looked over his shoulder.

His door was closed. Which was unusual. Mum and Dad always left it a little open. He hated it being closed. It made him feel scared.

He sat up, rubbing his eyes, thinking about opening it, though he hated walking on the floor in the dark. He knew it was silly, but he was worried that monsters would get him.

"Finally!" said a voice.

Whose voice was that?

He looked around his room, trying to find it.

"Over here you little fuck-brain."

It was a woman's voice, but it didn't sound like Mum's. It wasn't calm and soothing. It was harsh and gritty.

And then he saw her.

The outline of her body in the darkness, sitting on his chair in the corner.

"Jesus, took you long enough," she said.

His eyes opened wide. His body tensed.

Who was this woman?

He looked around his room.

Where was Mum and Dad?

Why weren't they helping him?

"Calm the fuck down," the woman said.

But Mikey couldn't calm down.

There was a strange woman in his room he didn't know, and she was using lots of bad words, and he couldn't understand what was going on.

He wanted her to leave. He wanted this to be over, whatever it was.

Was it a nightmare?

He pinched himself.

It hurt.

He was going red. He was hyperventilating. He couldn't breathe.

"We can't talk until you calm the fuck down. I mean, fuck, kid, you never had a stranger in your bedroom before?"

His breathing was quick. He was panting. Almost choking on his breath.

"My name is Joanna," she said.

"Mum!" he shouted. "Dad!"

"No use."

"Mum! Dad! Help!"

"I said it's no fucking use."

Her voice was angry and it made him shut up.

She held up a knife. A big one. It had a curved blade. She pointed it at him.

"They are not coming up here to save you," she said. "They are occupied."

Was she right?

Were they not coming?

"Mum!" he tried again. "Dad!"

"I said *quit it!* Or I'll gut you, you little shit."

He stopped shouting.

He didn't know what it meant to gut someone, but he knew it was bad.

"I want my Mum and Dad," he told her, his voice small.

"Of course you do. But they ain't coming."

"Why?"

"Because my boyfriend's brother is downstairs with a knife against your sister's throat."

Izzy. Were they going to hurt her?

"That gives us a bit of time to talk. Like I said while you were all yelling and shit – my name is Joanna. You can call me Jo or Joanna or whatever, don't care, all you need to know is that, if you do not do *exactly* as I say, I will kill you."

She leant forward.

"And when I say kill you, I don't just mean kill. I mean torture. I mean I will stick this knife in you and twist it around."

She demonstrated with the action of her knife.

"Then I will take it out and stick it back in, and twist it again. And you will scream. But it won't matter, because I'll just do it again. And I'll keep doing it until you stop moving because you're dead. Do you understand what I'm saying?"

He nodded.

She smiled and leant back.

"Brilliant. That means we can talk now. Are you ready to talk?"

Mikey looked at the door. Could he run?

"Don't think about it. I'll get to you before you reach it, and I will do exactly as I just said."

"What do you want?" he whimpered.

"Now that's a good question! See, we're on the right wave-length now. How great is that? You and me, see, we're connecting."

She smiled at him in a way that grown-ups do when they are trying to be reassuring.

"I want you to wait here until it's time."

"Time for what?"

She didn't answer the question.

She just grinned.

CHAPTER TWENTY-THREE

"Let her go," Noah said through gritted teeth.

Leon raised his eyebrows. As if Noah was a petulant child.

"They have nothing to do with this," Noah insisted. "It's me that defended Levi Isaacs. Not my family. Kill me if you have to, just leave them alone."

"Oh, stop being such a fucking martyr," Leon said. "You rich pricks are all the same – wanting to seem all honourable and shit. You got a killer piggy off, and you want to act all moral and that. You brought this on yourself."

"I know I did! That's my point, I brought it on me. You've had Michael, you have me, you don't need to–"

"I thought I told you to shut the fuck up and do as I say?"

"You did, I just wanted to say–"

Leon put the tip of his blade next to Izzy's throat.

"Stop it!"

Leon stood still. Not moving the knife. Just looking at Noah. Enjoying his suffering.

"Stop it, please!"

Leon didn't move.

"Get that knife away from my god damn child!"

Leon sniggered. "*God damn?* You rich arseholes can't even swear properly."

"She's just a baby, please!"

Leon sighed. "Noah, mate, I told you – you brought this on yourself." He dropped his knife to his side. "Declan, if you please."

Declan carried the baby past Noah.

"No!" Noah cried, reaching out for her, but Declan put his hand around Izzy's throat and Noah immediately retracted.

Noah was terrified this Declan guy would drop her. He did not seem stable. He barely seemed able to carry his own body, never mind the child. But here he was, walking chaotically, his limbs looking like they are working separately from each other, approaching the window.

Declan held Izzy in one hand, and opened the window with the other.

"What are you doing?"

Declan paused by the window and turned back to Leon. His face was like a child's, desperate for approval, enthusiastic to know he was doing well.

Leon was only too keen to appease him, saying, "Well done, Declan."

Noah went to object again, but feared what they may do. Instead, he just bowed his head. Closed his eyes. Hoped that, when he opened them again, this would not be happening.

He could feel Aubrey watching him. She'd said nothing so far. He couldn't tell if it was because she was too scared, or because she thought being obedient was the best option.

He opened his eyes again. Declan still had Izzy. By the window.

He shook his head. Willed away tears. Refused to show these people weakness, despite feeling so...

Feeble.

Both in his mind and in his body.

Feeble and pathetic.

He realised Leon was watching him. Grinning.

"There we are," Leon said. "I think you're beginning to understand, now – we are in charge."

Noah lifted his head. "What do you–"

"Ah, ah, ah!" Leon wagged his finger. "No talking."

Noah kept his mouth shut. Kept his eyes on Leon.

Refused to look at his daughter.

If he did, he would break.

"If you go against anything I say, Declan will hurl the shitbag out the window. If the impact doesn't kill her, the cold will."

Noah went to speak again, to affirm Leon's instructions, but didn't. Leon wanted him to remain silent, so he remained silent.

Compliant and submissive.

Just as Leon wanted him.

"Right. Now we understand each other, we can begin the first task."

Leon stepped out of the room, then came back in with a cricket bat, and an even wider grin.

Just at that moment, Izzy started crying.

CHAPTER TWENTY-FOUR

"Oh," Joanna said. "I do believe I can hear your sister."

It was coming from downstairs.

Mikey didn't understand, why was Izzy downstairs?

And there was a voice down there that he didn't know. It sounded gruff. Evil.

He realised his body was shaking. He felt cold and hot.

He began to cry.

"Oh, really?" Joanna said, raising an eyebrow.

She made him feel stupid, but he couldn't help it. He didn't mean to cry. He didn't want to. It was just happening. It was all too scary not to cry.

"Michael Logan's kid didn't do all this shit."

He dropped his head and buried it in his hands.

Izzy's crying grew louder, and so did his.

"Only little girls cry, you know."

She stood.

He kept his face buried in his hands. If he didn't see her, maybe she wasn't there.

"Even then, I never cried. And I was once a little girl."

He heard her move closer. She smelt like cigarettes and dirty clothes.

"Weak little children cry, Mikey. Pathetic little morsels who lack the courage to grow up. Is that you?"

Her hand ran up his leg, sending a shiver up and down his body. He flinched his leg away.

She gripped it.

Her hand was rough and coarse, and strong, and he couldn't move out of her grasp.

She sat down on the bed beside him.

"Look at me."

He shook his head.

"Look at me or I will cut your face."

He lifted his eyes from behind his hands. They were red and damp. Now he could see her face more closely, she looked even scarier. She had a tattoo by her eye. Two tear drops. They looked sore and new.

"What are you going to do?" he asked.

"What are we going to do?" She stuck her bottom lip out, pretended to think, then turned back to him. "We're going to torment your father. Rape your mother. Kill you in front of him. Then torture him to death. Probably in that order, but we'll see how things go."

Mikey didn't understand.

She leant toward him.

"Are you scared?" she whispered.

He nodded.

"Are you? Are you really?"

He nodded again, staring at the knife in her hand, resting casually on her lap.

"Let me tell you a secret."

She leaned even closer, her grip on his leg tightening, and placed her lips beside his ear. With the moisture of her cold breath brushing against his skin, she whispered gently, "You fucking should be."

She kissed him on the forehead, ruffled his hair, and stood.

She noticed a large wet patch spreading from his pyjama trousers and across the sheets.

She sniggered.

"You are fucking pathetic," she said.

CHAPTER TWENTY-FIVE

Aubrey watched her husband, her emotions so chaotic she was unable to discern one feeling from another. She was angry and terrified and tired and scared and vengeful and sad and resolute and in despair, all whilst also feeling numb. Shut off. Like these emotions had attacked her with such aggression she'd had to put up a wall to protect herself.

She wanted to say something. Anything.

But there was nothing she could say.

Noah had said it all. He was doing all he could.

But they had Izzy.

The strange-looking unstable one had Izzy, and he was standing by the window.

Why was he standing by the window?

What was he going to do?

And why didn't their phones work?

How had they managed to disable their damn phones?

Leon returned with a cricket bat, stretching with it behind his head, practising a few swings, all the while staring at Noah, grinning, enjoying his reaction.

"Here you go, Decs."

Leon threw his knife to Declan. Aubrey's breath caught as the knife sailed toward her baby, and Declan failed to catch it. She let her breath go, just for a moment, as the knife fell to the floor without doing any harm to Izzy. Declan picked up the knife and held it loosely as he cradled the crying child, and she struggled to breathe again.

Noah bowed his head, sobbing, muttering, "Please."

"As I said, Noah, this next task needs to go swimmingly, without any fuss from you. You understand?"

Noah didn't lift his head.

"I said, do you understand?"

"Fine," he said, quietly, a small utterance of a broken man.

Jesus. It's only taken ten minutes for them to destroy him.

She felt guilty for the thought, and reminded herself that she wouldn't do any better. She was doing what she thought she should do; be quiet. It felt like the responsibility was on Noah, but whatever he did, it would not be good enough.

She knew she wouldn't forgive Noah if he didn't protect their children, yet, at the same time, knew that whatever Noah did probably wouldn't be good enough.

"Stand up," Leon said.

Noah looked up at Leon, who placed the cricket bat on the underside of his throat and raised it up, bringing Noah to his feet.

"So what," Noah said, "you're going to kill me with a cricket bat?"

"Kill you?" Leon retorted. He looked at Roman and exchanged a snigger. "My friend, we're not ready to kill you yet. You're going to be the last to die."

Before Noah or Aubrey could register what Leon had just said, he swung the bat down, hard, against Noah's knee cap.

The echo of the impact made Aubrey flinch and Noah fell to his knees, howling.

She turned away. She couldn't watch this.

"Ah, ah, ah!" Leon said. "You make sure the bitch watches."

Roman pressed the tip of the blade against Aubrey's neck, grabbed her by the hair, and twisted her head so her gaze was directed at her husband. She knew she could close her eyes, but she didn't dare.

She did not want to suffer the same pain they were putting Noah through.

"And you," Leon said to Noah. "I want you on your feet."

Noah resisted, at first. Then he looked at Izzy. Wailing in the corner, held by a mad man, and that was all the motivation either of them needed.

Once again, Leon placed the edge of the bat beneath Noah's chin and lifted it as Noah rose.

"Please," Noah said. "I don't–"

Leon swung the bat again, landing it against the other kneecap, and Noah fell to his knees with a cry of anguish.

Aubrey went to look away, then remembered she wasn't supposed to. She stared at her husband as he endured the pain.

She'd seen her husband suffer in their many years of marriage. The death of his father, the troubles when Izzy was born, the ethical implications of his job – she had witnessed him overcome torment after torment.

She was not sure if she could watch him overcome this one.

CHAPTER TWENTY-SIX

There was no word for the pain.

Excruciating may come close, but it wasn't close enough.

Noah looked at Izzy again. His reminder. His reason for doing what this sick bastard told him to.

He felt pathetic. Humiliated. And lost.

Completely lost.

But mostly, he felt shocks of pain rushing up and down his legs.

"Stand. Up."

Noah did as Leon said, his legs wobbling, allowing the cricket bat to bring him to his feet again.

This time, he closed his eyes and winced, knowing what was to come. His kneecaps were throbbing, but it didn't matter to Leon. Leon swung the cricket bat again, causing an audible crack upon impact, and Noah squirmed on the floor

"Get up," Leon said.

Noah went to get up, but Leon didn't wait this time. He swung the bat, thwacking it against Noah's kneecap. And again. And again. And again.

He rolled back and forth, writhing, tears forming in the corners of his eyes. But he didn't cry. He refused. But he still couldn't help but wail in agony.

Leon stopped for a moment and stood back, allowing Noah to feel the aftermath.

"Stand. Up."

Noah looked up at Leon. He couldn't be serious.

Noah wasn't sure his legs would lift him, never mind support his weight. Not after that.

Leon raised his eyebrows and looked at Izzy.

With a groan, Noah pushed up on his hands and tried to steady himself. Leon stood back, enjoying the performance, exchanging looks of mirth with Roman.

Noah managed to balance himself, but his legs were shaking, wobbling too hard, and he had to hold his arms out to try to retain his balance.

Leon walked up to Noah's side, pausing by his ear, so close Noah could feel the heat of his breath.

He said, "You may want to close your eyes for this one."

Noah slowly swivelled his head. Looked into Leon's eyes. Up close, he just looked like a child. A kid who knew nothing. A thug. A bully.

"I'm sorry about your brother," Noah said.

Leon's grin immediately disappeared.

"It was sad what happened. Awful. And I shouldn't have defended that police officer."

Leon licked his lips. Noah could see the fury, could see every pore sweating, could see every flicker and flinch of constrained anger.

"But your brother wouldn't want you to do this. I know that."

Leon shook his head. "That's where you're wrong." Leon stood back and held the bat out, getting as much swing as he could. "This is *exactly* what Jamal would have wanted me to do."

Noah shook his head.

He knew what was coming.

He knew what Leon was doing.

And he cried. He hated himself for it, but he cried as he looked into the eyes of his assailant and saw no mercy.

Then he looked at Izzy.

And he knew he had no choice.

Leon swung the bat into Noah's knee, and the crack was louder than his scream, audible to everyone in the room as his knee bent backwards.

Noah didn't see his wife flinching, but he heard her gasp.

He fell to the ground. Tried clutching it, but every touch just added to the already immense amount of pain.

He couldn't stand up now even if he wanted to. His leg was broken.

He had no chance at all.

CHAPTER TWENTY-SEVEN

The cry was loud enough to be heard from Mikey's room. Was that Dad?

What had they done to him?

Joanna grinned, smacking her hands together, practically dancing.

"Damn!" she said. "My boy's got a hell of a swing, don't he?"

Mikey's cheeks were wet. His pyjamas were wet. His sheets were wet.

And this woman would not stop smiling and laughing and Mikey wondered, he wondered, desperately wondered, what she was going to do to him.

"That was your dad, by the way," Joanna said. "My boy is beating the shit out of him."

She sat close to him on the bed, and he tried to crawl away, but she put her hand on his throat and her grip was so tight that he couldn't go anywhere.

Then she loosened her grip, let go, and stroked his hair. In the way Mum sometimes did. But it wasn't affectionate like when Mum did it. It was gentle, but it felt wrong.

Like she wasn't doing it out of love, but out of something else. Something worse.

Something far, far worse.

"It sucks that we have to be up here, don't it? I'd love to be with my boy, watching him work. It's arousing, you know?"

She kept stroking his hair.

He wished she'd stop.

"Well, obviously, you don't know. What are you, six? Seven? Eight?"

"I'm eleven."

"Fuck me, boy, you're short. Well small for your age. What are you, retarded?"

He didn't understand what that meant.

"I mean, don't worry, our Declan is too. You'll meet him. He's the one with Izzy."

Izzy? What were they doing to Izzy?

"Lie down."

He stared at her.

Why did she want him to lie down?

"Don't you understand me? I said lie down."

She held her knife out. Not putting it against his skin, but showing it to him. Twisting it proudly. Letting him know the threat was always there.

"You fucking hear me?"

He laid down.

"Roll over."

He went to roll toward her, but she said, "Other way you little shit," and he turned over so his back was to her.

Then he felt her lie behind him. She moved close, so he could feel her knees in the back of his, her waist against his waist, her breasts in his back.

And she tucked her arm around him, holding him close.

Her knife remained in her hand as she held him close, and he stared at it, unable to keep his focus on anything else.

"Don't worry," she whispered into his ear. "My boy will call us down soon. It won't be too long now."

He waited for her to say something else, but she didn't, and he just stared at his toy chest in the corner.

Silence descended, and they just lay there.

His entire body shaking.

Yet, the more he shook, the more she pulled him close, and the more she whispered in his ear that it was going to be okay, the more he was sure it wasn't.

And the sounds got worse.

Dad's voice. Shouting. Moaning. Crying.

Pleading.

And Joanna, chuckling quietly beneath it all.

"Ah," she said. "Don't you just love the sound of imminent death?"

Then she was silent again, and he was forced to listen.

CHAPTER TWENTY-EIGHT

The lampshade that Noah had picked out with Aubrey at Ikea when they first moved in – the one that they fell out over, which made Aubrey upset because she realised she'd become the crying woman in Ikea that they'd always smirked at – *that* lampshade turned into a spinning mess, the red flowers melding into the blurs of the green flowers and the white of the background.

Pain shot up and down his leg. He'd never broken anything before, not even so much as fractured a bone. It was pain he couldn't describe.

He went to touch his leg, but as soon as his hand went near his skin, the pain intensified, and his leg wobbled, and he cried out.

His leg was unusable. He couldn't run. He couldn't fight. What use was he to his family now?

These people didn't want money. They didn't want to reason with him. They wanted revenge.

In a strange way, Noah understood it. He'd want revenge too. But he'd never even consider breaking into someone's house and breaking their legs.

Then again, as far as these people were concerned, he was just a rich upper-middle class man. What the hell did he know about pain?

He'd always thought he was lucky.

Now he realised he was hated.

Leon's ominous figure moved through the spinning, blurred lines of the room, and towered over Noah.

Noah rolled over. Groaned.

Refused to pass out.

If he passed out, who knew what he would wake up to.

Amongst all the pain, he hadn't looked at Izzy. She was still in the hands of the strange guy. Still with a blade by her throat.

"Fine," Noah said. "You've got me. What now?"

Leon didn't move. His blurred figure loomed over Noah. Noah had no idea what expression was on his face.

"What's next in the plan, huh?" Noah tried to sound confident, but was too aware of the pain to avoid the agony coming through in his voice. "Are you going to set fire to my house? Burn me alive? Kill my children? Huh?"

Leon sniggered. As did Roman. They muttered something about how Noah was actually fairly accurate.

"You're a bunch of psychos," he said, figuring he had nothing to lose by saying it. He thought that they had inflicted as much pain as they could. He thought it wouldn't matter, that there was little more they could do.

Oh, how wrong he was.

Leon crouched down. Slowly, his face came into focus. Then out of focus. Then back in focus. He blurred back and forth, like a camera lens that couldn't quite decide where to focus its attention.

"Us?" Leon said, his voice low and husky. "We're the psychos?"

"Yes. You. All of you, you bloody cretins."

"Cretins? What's that, a posh word for bad man?"

"Go to Hell."

"You see, Noah, Jamal was a nice guy. He was killed by the filth for going five miles an hour over the limit. You got that pig off. You let him go free."

Leon grabbed hold of Noah's face, squeezing his cheeks, and Noah could see the aggression increasing, could feel it intensifying, and he knew he'd said the wrong thing.

"Only a sick fuck could take pride in helping a murderer get off."

Leon stood.

"It was my job," Noah whimpered. "It was–"

Leon slammed the heel of his boot down upon Noah's face. His nose cracked, and he was forced to breathe through his mouth as his nostrils filled with blood.

"Well this is my job," Leon said. "Look at it that way, and maybe we'll understand each other."

Leon wiped his boot on Noah's shirt, leaving streaks of his blood over the ironed silk.

Noah looked up. Saw Aubrey behind him. On her knees. Shaking. Sobbing silently. Unable to avoid crying, but not willing to make a sound as she did it.

God, she was terrified.

And what could he do about it?

She looked back at him, and looked helpless, and he felt bad, then realised; he looked just the same.

Then he turned his head to the window. Declan still held Izzy, the knife hanging loosely in the hand supporting the baby's head.

Surely they wouldn't hurt a baby?

Surely no one could be that monstrous?

Noah went to speak. Then the doorbell went, and he felt a tinge of hope.

CHAPTER TWENTY-NINE

This wasn't unexpected.

In fact, Leon was prepared for such an eventuality, and he trusted in the power he had over this family.

At first, he looked at Noah's eyes, staring back at him from his beaten, bruised position on the floor. Pathetic little man. Barely a man, really. Leon took beatings when he was a boy, whether from the bigger kids at school or from his mother's latest boyfriend. He had never just laid down and taken it. They'd always had something back, even if he lost in the end.

The doorbell rang again.

Leon looked at Aubrey. Noah's whore. A mixture of hope and terror in her face.

"You're going to answer the door," he declared.

Aubrey's breath caught in her throat. Leon could see the conundrums passing through her thoughts. Should she signal to this person? Should she run? Should she beg them to help?

Or would she shut the hell up so her family could live?

"If you so much as hint, or give any signal to whoever it is, do you know what I'll do?"

He stepped toward Aubrey. Towering over her. Casting her in his shadow.

She knew the answer, but he was going to give it to her anyway.

"I will gut your husband. I will slit your baby's throat. Then I will go upstairs and open your boy's chest. Do you understand?"

She didn't move. Her eyes were wide. Those eyes had never seen anything so terrible. This rich bitch was probably so averse to violence that she couldn't even watch films where bad things happen.

She hadn't had to grow up fighting, and that was why she was so submissive.

"I need an answer, Aubrey. Do you understand?"

She nodded, slowly.

"Perfect."

"Noah?" came a woman's voice through the door. "Aubrey? Are you in there? Is everything all right?"

Noah turned to Aubrey and said, "It's Verity Cunningham."

Leon grinned. "The local MP, huh?"

"She couldn't do anything even if you did signal to her," Noah told Aubrey, the pain in his voice audible. "She's a clueless lady. Just get rid of her, please."

"Hear that?" Leon said to Aubrey. "She's clueless. Are you going to do as your husband says?"

She paused, thought about it, then faintly nodded.

"Beautiful. Time you opened the door then, yeah?"

She nodded again, then stood. Shook her arms. Looked from her husband to Leon, to her baby, then walked in tiny steps toward the front door.

CHAPTER THIRTY

P*lease, help us.*
Please, they are going to kill us.
Please, just phone the police.

Those were a few of the things Aubrey wished she could say.

Maybe she could wink. Widen her eyes. Give some kind of signal.

But Noah was right. Verity wasn't able to take a hint. She'd brought a revolting lasagne round to wish Noah good luck for leaving his job – she was hardly the most head-screwed-on kind of person. Even the constituents who voted for her did so on the pretence that she was simply a better option than her opponents, who were equally clueless and even more sheltered by their privilege.

So she walked toward the door, taking it small step by small step, staring at the handle she was about to turn.

She placed a hand on it.

Closed her eyes.

Took a deep breath.

Looked behind her. Through the living room doorway she

could see a glimpse of Noah's deformed leg. The stairs were behind her, leading to her son.

This was going to be tough. Not just getting rid of this woman – but doing so without pleading for help.

But it was for the good of the family.

She opened the door. Marginally. Just enough for her face and body to be visible.

Verity stood on the porch, her cardigan wrapped around her. It was beige and ugly, and she hated it.

"Hi, Verity," Aubrey said, trying to make her voice sound as relaxed as it could, as if she'd just been woken up.

"Oh my gosh, were you sleeping?"

"No. Well, yes. Kind of. We were watching a film and I fell asleep."

"Oh dear. Bad film?"

"I can't even remember. I think Mikey liked it."

"I imagine it probably had robots or guns in it then!"

"I think so." Aubrey forced a fake chuckle, hoping it didn't come across as too fake. "What can I do for you?"

"Well, I brought a lasagne along earlier. To wish Noah good luck for leaving his job."

"Yes, he did say."

"Did you have it for tea? How was it?"

"We, er… No. We were saving it."

"Oh, well you best eat it tomorrow then. Don't want it to go off."

"Of course not."

"I was just hoping to get the dish back, but I suppose you won't have finished with it yet."

"Not quite yet."

Verity's eyes narrowed, and she stared intently at Aubrey.

"Is everything okay, dear?" she asked.

"I – well – what do you mean?"

"I don't know. Something just seems… off."

"No. I, erm… I'm just tired."

"Is everything okay with Noah?"

"Noah's fine."

"He's not hurting you, is he?"

"Why would he be…"

Verity pointed to Aubrey's t-shirt. There was a drop of blood. It must be Noah's. Perhaps it had landed on her while they were beating him.

"Oh, that's…" She tried to think of something, quickly. "Probably Mikey's. He had a nosebleed earlier."

"Are you sure?"

"Yes. It's okay, I just need to put it in the wash."

"You don't have to protect anyone, you know that. If someone is hurting you… You can say."

Aubrey wished this woman would just go. As good as her intentions were, she knew this would just be part of tomorrow's gossip. *Noble lawyer beats wife.*

"I promise you, everything is fine."

"I've heard those words before, Aubrey. Then the women who said them ended up dead a few months later."

"Honestly, Verity, it's late, and I just want to get back inside and go to bed."

Even though she was attempting to be rude, this didn't dissuade her. In fact, Verity leant to the side, trying to see past Aubrey, further into the house.

"Mrs Cunningham, please, we will have your lasagne dish for you tomorrow."

Verity leant back, looked Aubrey up and down, and nodded.

"If you're sure, dear."

"Yep."

"Okay, good night."

"Good night," Aubrey said, and shut the door.

CHAPTER THIRTY-ONE

"**I**f you're sure, dear."

Noah heard Verity's words amongst the silence of the room, everyone straining to listen to the conversation.

She was such a clueless woman. Believing Noah had hurt Aubrey. He wasn't sure it was possible for someone to misinterpret a situation quite so drastically.

"Yep."

"Okay, good night."

"Good night."

The front door closed.

And with it, a hope of escape.

Noah was glad Aubrey hadn't said or done anything reckless. He was pleased they had all survived this part of the ordeal.

But he was also a little disappointed. Someone other than Verity, and they may have actually realised the family was in danger.

But not Verity.

Never Verity.

Aubrey returned to the room and Leon clapped his hands.

Loud claps made with gestures to emphasise his point.

"Well done you!" he said. "You did so well. You did."

Leon turned to Noah and said, "Didn't she do well?"

Noah made eye contact with Aubrey and held it. No words were spoken, but he could feel their understanding. The knowledge that they'd taken a risk, and they hoped it paid off.

"What now?" Noah said to Leon. His legs were shaking and throbbing. He was getting used to the pain, but that didn't mean it was any less agonising.

"What do you mean, what now?"

"What else do you want?"

"What else do I want?"

"I can't walk! You've scared my wife, my kids – you've made your point. Now what do you want from us?"

"You think this is it? You think this is all we have planned?"

"I don't see what else you wish to–"

"You think a little bit of torment makes up for freeing my brother's killer?"

"Your brother's killer? If he'd have just let the police officer arrest him–"

"Then what? Have you ever been arrested, Noah?"

Leon stood over Noah, sneering, his face becoming less and less sadistically playful, and more overtly ruthless.

"No," Noah replied.

"You sit there saying, 'oh, if that was me, I would have just given myself up,' or, 'if I had done nothing wrong then why fight' – but it's never been you, Noah. Has it?"

"I get your point."

"I don't think you do. You can afford lawyers that will stop it even going to trial." Leon started chuckling. "You know the worst part? They thought my brother was homeless, or on drugs. The press didn't even care."

"I don't see why that's relevant–"

"You wouldn't, would you? Because it's never been you. And it will *never* be you."

Noah looked down and moaned, then looked back up. This man had an agenda, and nothing Noah said would be good enough. Leon was pissed off about his lot in life, and it was Noah who was going to feel the brunt of it.

"Fine," Noah said. "Fine, you win. You had things harder than me. Now will you let my family go?"

Leon smiled at Declan, who started rocking Izzy back and forth, more and more furiously.

"He's going to hurt her," Noah said. He drowned out the sound of Aubrey begging him to stop.

"I said he's going to hurt her!" Noah repeated.

Declan rocked their baby harder.

"You have me, okay! Now let my baby go!"

"Let her go?" Leon repeated.

"Yes. Please."

Leon raised his eyebrows and looked to Declan. He looked, for a moment, that he was actually considering letting the baby go free.

Noah's heart leapt. They had a chance.

"You heard the man," Leon said. "Let the baby go."

Noah, for the first time, felt hopeful that these people weren't going to hurt his daughter.

Then Declan opened the window, threw the baby like a rugby ball, and she disappeared into the night.

CHAPTER THIRTY-TWO

"No!" Aubrey screamed.

She could no longer stay silent.

Her self-control was as battered as her husband's legs.

What had they just done?

"*Izzy!*"

Leon grinned at her as Declan shut and locked the window.

"You fucking prick! You arsehole! *Izzy!*"

"Hey, Roman, mate – you want to shut that bitch up?"

She leapt from her place on the floor, out of Roman's grasp, feeling his fingers trace her back, leapt over Noah, shoved Declan out of the way and reached the window.

"*Izzy!*"

She searched and searched, but her eyes couldn't see her baby anywhere. There was a bush just outside the window, maybe she'd landed in there? Maybe it had cushioned Izzy's fall, and she was okay?

Aubrey looked back and forth.

Then she looked again.

No sign.

She banged against the window, shouting her daughter's name over and over, "Izzy! *Izzy!*" but she couldn't hear her.

The baby wasn't even crying.

If she was hurt, or distressed, or even alone, she would cry.

But she wasn't making a damn sound.

She had to get out there.

She had to.

She had to get to her baby.

She turned back to the men watching her. Noah on the floor, weeping, trying to push himself up but unable to.

Declan looking back at her, then at Leon, then to the ground. He couldn't stay still. He was always twitching, always looking.

Roman, flexing his fingers over the handle of his knife.

And Leon. Stood in the doorway. Arms folded. Watching her with that same smug, expectant expression.

"Please," Aubrey said.

"Excuse me?" Leon said, cupping his ear.

"Please. Just let me–"

"Let you what?"

"Let me get out there. Let me check she's okay. Please."

Leon's grin spread even wider. "Wow. It's not often I have a rich bitch pleading with me."

"I *don't care* how much *fucking money you have!*"

Her voice broke. She hated that she was a cliché. She was the hysterical woman whose every shout was a scream, and she despised herself for it, but that's what she was doing – screaming. And it was with such ferociousness that her throat struggled to handle it.

"That piggy cared," Leon said.

"Piggy? What's a piggy? I don't care!"

"Piggy's called Levi Isaacs. Police officer. The nice man who killed my brother."

"I'm not him!"

Leon shook his head. "You're all him. Or as good as."

"Piss off! I support Help For Heroes, I donated to the homeless charity, I did all that! I am not like that!"

Leon smirked at Roman, then gave a few slow, sarcastic claps.

"Well done! You posted a few hashtags, shared a few posts, gave a few quid, and that forgives you for everything?"

"Everything? For what, what have I done?"

"A few hundred years of hypocrisy to start with."

"Hey, guess what – that wasn't me! I'm not responsible for what well-off people have done throughout history! It's something that happened, and has no bearing on anything right now!"

"Oh, and what, you cross me in the street with my hood up and these tattoos and you're saying you don't assume I'm a criminal?"

And then it came out. The proverbial nail in the coffin. The words that sealed her fate, the ones she knew she shouldn't say, but they passed her lips anyway:

"But you *are* a criminal."

Leon said nothing. Just allowed the words to hang in the room, letting them speak for him.

"Please just let me get to my baby," she said.

Leon stayed silent. His expression blank, looking back at her, neither caring for her nor her child.

"Please."

No reaction.

"Please, just…"

Not even a blink.

"For fuck's sake! It's freezing out there and she may have landed on her head, let me check if my *damn baby* is *okay!*"

Nothing.

Still, nothing.

"I am going out there," she said decisively, standing tall,

gathering all the courage she could. "You can try to stop me if you wish, but there is nothing you can do that will stop me from going to check if my baby is alive."

"You think?" Leon said.

Aubrey's lip curled. Her face stiffened. She wasn't backing down.

"You so much as try to get out of this room and we'll slit your eldest's throat."

Aubrey frowned.

Her eldest?

Oh, God.

How could she not have thought?

Mikey ...

"Oh, Joanna!" Leon called.

"Coming!" replied a woman's voice, and the sound of Mikey's bedroom door creaking open forced Aubrey to remain rooted to the spot.

CHAPTER THIRTY-THREE

"Coming!" Joanna shouted, then turned to Mikey with a smile so eager it was terrifying.

"That's our cue!" she said, bouncing around, jigging excitedly. "Get up!"

He didn't want to get up.

He didn't want to go with her.

He wanted her to leave.

"I said get up," she said, her teeth gritted. She reached across the bed and put the knife next to his throat. "Or I'll spray your blood all over these walls."

He climbed out of bed, crying. He felt silly because he was too old to cry, and he was too old to wet his pyjamas, but he couldn't help it. He wanted Mum and Dad, and he wanted them now.

She led him out of the room and into the dark, foreboding hallway. She held onto the back of his pyjamas, scrunching the material, and dragged him downstairs, her knife remaining by his throat.

She led him into the living room, and his heart leapt at the sight of Mum and Dad, and he hoped that they could help him.

Except they couldn't.

Dad was on the floor. Staring up at Mikey with a lost look; a strange mixture of pain entwined with terror. His legs were spread out at strange angles.

Mum was by the window. Staring at him with her hands over her mouth.

"Mum!"

She move toward him, but Joanna pulled him back and pressed the tip of the blade against his throat, and she halted.

There were three other people there too. An odd-looking man in the corner. Another man who looked big and muscular. And another man who sat in Dad's chair with his leg hanging over the arm.

"Come over here," the man said to him.

Mikey looked to Mum. To Dad. Should he do what they say?

"I said come over here," the man said again.

Joanna shoved him forward, and he had no choice but to walk toward him.

"I'm Leon. And you are?"

Mikey rubbed his eyes. Looked at his parents again.

"Stop looking at them," said Leon. "They aren't going to help you. I'm talking to you. What's your name?"

"Mikey."

"Mikey. Sit on my lap, Mikey."

Mikey really didn't want to.

"Sit on it or I'll cut your throat."

He cried harder, and kept crying as he perched on Leon's knee. Mikey felt the blade of Leon's knife resting against his belly.

"What do you think?" Leon asked Joanna as she leant against the door frame, surveying the room.

"It's beautiful," she said. "Fucking beautiful."

"Please just let him go," Mum said. "You don't need to hurt my children."

"It's time for you to go back on your knees now," Leon told her.

Mum's face scrunched up, like she was praying or trying not to cry like Mikey was.

The muscular man walked over to her, collected her, and took her to the space beside Dad, where he pushed her to her knees and placed the knife against her throat.

She did not stop staring at Mikey, and he did not stop staring at her. It made him feel both better and worse. She was here, which was good – but she was letting it happen. All of it.

They were bullying her too.

"You've got what you came for," Dad said. "You've battered me. You've harassed my wife and hurt my children. Kill me if you want, but please be done. It's enough."

"I'm getting a little tired of the begging now, Noah," said Leon. "It needs to stop, or I start hurting people."

"Start?"

"Yes, start. You ain't seen nothing yet. You've had your turn. So has your baby. Now it's hers."

He turned to look at Aubrey.

"Oh, God," she said, and looked down.

"Don't worry, we're not going to beat your legs," Leon reassured her. "We are going to have much more fun than that."

She whimpered as she shook her head. Her cheeks were red and damp, just like Mikey's.

Leon left a silence lingering in the room, then finally broke it. "Tell your husband who *he* is."

"What?" snapped Aubrey. "Tell him who what is?"

"Your husband. Tell him who *he* is."

"Who?"

"Aubrey, I feel you know exactly what I'm saying. Stop being difficult or I will start breaking things."

"I don't know who *he* is. Please, tell me and then I'll do whatever you want."

"Fine." Leon ran a hand over Mikey's hair, looked at Dad's pained, clueless expression, then back to Mum.

"Graham," he finally said. "Tell your husband who Graham is."

CHAPTER THIRTY-FOUR

A ubrey turned and looked into her husband's wide, innocent eyes.

He had the same eyes as Mikey. Izzy had her eyes, but Noah's were Mikey's. They both looked as desperately helpless as each other's. So empty of faith.

Leon was forcing those eyes to break.

No. Not like this.

She wasn't sure she'd have ever told Noah the truth, but if she had, this would certainly have not been the moment.

"It's fine," Noah said, his voice stern and reassuring. She hated that. "Just tell me whatever it is they want you to tell me."

His sincerity brought more tears to her eyes. He was being understanding because he had to. The only reaction worse than anger is indifference.

"If this is all they need you to do, then just do it," Noah said. "Tell me. It won't matter."

She looked down and tried to find the words. Once she found them, she tried to push them out, but they remained in her mind, getting more and more jumbled in every moment.

"Hear that?" Leon interrupted. "He said he won't care. I mean, he will, but he said he won't. So you may as well break it to him."

They both ignored him

Aubrey shook her head, closed her eyes and, in the quietest voice she could manage, she said, "I had an affair."

"We can't hear you!" Leon said.

"I said I had an affair!" she repeated, louder, then to avoid looking at her husband, she turned to Leon and asked, "happy?"

"I'd ask your husband that."

She turned back to Noah. She wanted to know where Izzy was. She wanted them to take the knife away from Mikey's neck. And she wanted to avoid her dying words being an admission of adultery.

"I'm sorry," Aubrey said, though it felt stupid in the current situation.

She could see Noah was hurt. She could see it in his face. But he was refusing to let it show, refusing to let it get the better of him. They both knew what Leon was doing, but she also knew that Noah would put any resentment aside for the sake of their survival.

At least, she hoped.

"Tell him more."

Aubrey turned toward Leon, trying to ignore his son's stare, and snapped, "What exactly do you want me to tell him?"

"How long, maybe?"

She glared at Leon.

"And we'll know if you're lying," Leon assured her. "And we'll kill your son if you do. So I'd avoid telling any porkies."

"Fine." She turned back to Noah and stated, matter-of-factly, "Three Years."

She saw his eyes widen, and saw him resist the impulse to react.

"How did you meet him?" Leon asked.

"He was someone I dated before I met you."

"And are the kids your husband's?"

"Yes, they are! They are his!"

Leon shrugged. "Just asking, you never know."

She turned to apologise to Noah again, but didn't. She wasn't sure why. It just felt like there were more important things.

Noah took a deep breath and let it go.

"It's fine," Noah said. "Let's just... it's fine."

"Noah..."

She wanted to say that they needed to be a team.

That they couldn't be divided.

That they couldn't let this stop them from losing their family.

But none of it sounded right.

"Right now, I don't care," Noah said, looking at no one but Leon. "Right now, I just want to know if Izzy is okay, and get my wife and Mikey out of here."

"How honourable," Leon interjected. "Well, seeing as your wife is such a slut, I think we should all see what it is Graham liked so much."

She glared at Leon. "I thought I was done. I thought that's all you wanted from me."

He shook his head. "I never said that."

"Yes, you did."

"I said I wouldn't break anything. I didn't say that was all you had to do. That would be a pretty shit punishment, wouldn't it?"

"Punishment?"

"Come on, take it off. Hurry and I promise I won't let my boner touch your son."

She looked to her child again.

"Or I could just cut his throat."

Aubrey would have thought they'd grown tired of threatening their lives by now. She'd have thought the words would have lost meaning.

They hadn't.

Because Aubrey believed them.

After what they had done to Noah and Izzy, she believed them entirely.

"Fine," she said, and went to take her top off.

"Ah, ah, ah!" Leon said, wagging his finger. "Stand up. Let us all see the goods."

Her lips pursed. Her fists clenched.

She thought of Izzy laying outside, cold and alone.

Of Mikey with the knife by his throat.

And she stood.

"And then what?" she asked. "I take my clothes off, then what? Is there more?"

"Let's just begin with the clothes, shall we? Then we'll go from there."

She looked at Noah. He was looking the other way.

Aubrey pulled her top over her head, revealing a white, plain bra.

Joanna whooped and clapped. Roman laughed. Declan fidgeted uncomfortably.

And Leon leant ever so slightly forward.

She paused, glared at him, and he raised his eyebrows, prompting her to continue.

She was just getting undressed. That's all it was.

Just getting undressed for bed, or to go in the shower.

She was alone, getting undressed, and this was not as humiliating as it felt.

She pushed her trousers down, revealing matching white panties, equally plain.

"Wow," Leon said. "Look at those panties. I guess that's what happens when you're married, huh? No more fancy underwear."

She closed her eyes and shook her head. She couldn't let him get to her.

"Or is it Graham who gets the fancy underwear?"

She wrapped her arms around her chest, covering her breasts, and felt Roman's fingers running gently down her back.

She stepped away from his hand.

"Well, we're waiting." Leon prompted.

She scowled. "For what?"

He waved his hand, indicating for her to continue.

She shook her head. "You can't be serious?"

He dragged his knife down Mikey's arm, tearing his pyjamas and leaving a line of blood. Mikey howled, tears streaming down his cheek, and she had to resist the urge to run to her son and cradle him as Leon moved the knife to his throat.

"I'm getting tired of having to ask twice."

"Mummy…" Mikey whimpered.

"It's okay, darling," she whispered. "It's all going to be okay."

Leon grinned. "You shouldn't lie to your son."

"Fuck you!"

He said nothing. He didn't need to. He knew he was in control.

"Please, Aubrey," said her husband's soft voice, his face still turned away, still unable to watch. "Just do what they say."

She reached behind her bra, unclasped it, and let it slide down her arms and onto the floor, then covered her petite breasts with her arms.

A beat went by and Leon said, "You know what I'm going to ask next."

She huffed, freed one of her arms from covering her chest, pushed her panties to her feet, and stepped out of them.

Leon cheered. "Wow! Didn't take you for a Brazilian kinda woman, but look at that!"

She went to cover herself.

"Drop your arms."

She looked at him pleadingly.

"I said drop them," he repeated.

She did as she was told, unveiling her body to the room. Joanna gave a low-pitch, sinister chuckle while Roman licked his lips, smirking, and Leon eagerly looked her up and down.

Her son cried even harder. Noah was the only one who didn't look.

Leon stood and pushed Mikey into Joanna's arms. Aubrey reached out for her son, almost stroking his fingers, but Joanna wrapped her arms around Mikey before Aubrey was able, embracing him in a suffocating hug. Like it was affectionate whilst not being affectionate at all. Joanna's psychotic intentions masked by faux kindness.

Leon said to Roman, "Anyone moves, kill them."

Roman nodded.

Leon walked to the dining room door. He opened it.

"In here," he told Aubrey.

"No, please…"

Joanna scraped her finger down Mikey's wound, and he cried out, and her heart stopped for a moment.

Leon didn't need to ask again.

Aubrey dropped her head and shuffled pathetically away from her family and into the dining room.

Leon shut the door behind them.

CHAPTER THIRTY-FIVE

Noah kept his eyes closed,
It was almost silent at first. Just an undercurrent of shuffling, of Joanna's arms around his son, the twitching of Declan, and the fidgeting of Roman, standing over him; as if he needed a minder. He couldn't walk. He couldn't get up. He couldn't resist if he wished.

Then the noises started.

It was Leon to begin with. Loud, manly grunting. Excessive. Deliberate.

Leon didn't need to make this much noise. Noah knew it was all for him.

The grunting grew louder, and Noah tried to go numb to it.

Tried to fight off the images.

Tried to resist the pain; both the mental torture and the physical anguish. All of it. In his legs, in his mind, in his heart... Every bit of agony they had inflicted upon him, spilling into his thoughts like an overflowing bucket rocking from side to side.

He finally reached a place where he could block it out.

Then Aubrey's voice joined in.

Not with the happy moans or screams of aggressive pleasure that Leon was projecting.

These were screams of terror.

Aubrey didn't like it rough. She liked it slow. She liked to make love, to be tender.

Noah did not imagine that Leon was being tender. Noah imagined he was thrusting his cock inside of her as far as he could, and as hard as he could. This was not about his pleasure; it was solely about her pain.

Her screams increased, mixed with cries. She didn't plead, say stop, say no, but she shouted, audible shrieks merging with Leon's pleasure.

Leon grew louder and louder until he reached the peak and let out one long, big scream, and Aubrey's screeches turned into a high-pitched squeal.

Then silence.

Too much silence.

There was no movement. Nothing. No one in the room said or did anything.

They just let the silence linger.

Noah opened his eyes. Looked up at Joanna, feeling her eyes on him. She was grinning, with something sick and twisted in her eyes.

"He's my man," she said. "He likes it hard and fast. I promise she'd have had a good time."

He almost asked, *and you are okay with him fucking another woman*, then realised just how stupid it would sound. As if, after everything they had done, they would care about infidelity.

Then he caught a glimpse of Mikey, who also stared at him, crying without making a sound. The poor kid didn't dare make any noise. Joanna muttered in his ear any time he made a sound that she would gut him if he dared.

The door to the dining room opened.

Noah tried to peer inside. Tried to see Aubrey. He caught a quick glimpse of her bare buttocks and the red marks left upon them as Leon walked out, doing up his flies and his belt.

He nodded approvingly at Noah.

"Tight," he said. "Especially after two kids. Got a good one there."

He looked at Roman.

"Your turn."

"No!" Noah cried out. He hadn't meant to; it just came out. "Please, no more!"

They ignored him, and Roman rushed into the dining room like a child rushing downstairs on Christmas morning, and shut the door behind him.

Leon sat back in his seat.

"Look, if you–" Noah went to say.

Leon lifted a hand and silenced him.

"Not right now," Leon said. "I really want to listen to this."

CHAPTER THIRTY-SIX

Aubrey's breasts pressed against the dining table, her body aching. Aside from her vigorous shaking, she didn't move. A soreness throbbed inside of her, like a hand with sharp nails had reached in and scraped down her cervix.

She didn't even look up when Roman entered the room.

Why bother?

She knew what was coming. She had to go numb.

But as soon as he thrust himself inside of her, she knew it would be impossible. Leon's aggressive thrusts had left her tender, and Roman was rubbing the exact places that felt on fire. After every penetration, she released a breath of relief, then cried out as the next thrust only exacerbated the agony.

She tried not to cry out, she really did. She knew it was what they wanted. She knew it would only spur Roman on, and she knew that everyone in the living room could hear her, her voice melding with the hyperbolic grunts of her aggressors.

But there was nothing she could do to stop herself.

She had never known pain like it. This wasn't how sex was,

or had ever been for her. Ever since she was young, when a man might show even the smallest bit of force, it would hurt, and she'd ask them to slow down. She hadn't disliked the notion of rough sex, it was just that, in practise, it hurt her.

Now these men were penetrating her in ways she not only wasn't used to, but couldn't handle.

Roman's screams grew more frequent and, once again, she felt his penis throb in the same way that Leon's did, and he went faster and it hurt more and he grabbed her side, pulling what little loose skin she had and gripping it between his nails, pinching her.

Just as he reached his crescendo and her pain intensified, she lifted her face, and her eyes widened.

And she saw it.

Displayed in the cabinet beside the dining table. The knife. The ceremonial dagger. Noah's family heirloom.

The athame.

If she could get to it…

If she could somehow reach it…

In a moment he would be in post-orgasmic bliss. She could take advantage. Use the moment when he's off-guard and not expecting this submissive woman to fight back.

He finished, but did not pull out. He leant over her, leaning his hands on her back, pressing her breasts harder against the table where she and her son had eaten every evening for the past decade.

Her eyes wandered past the cabinet, to the pictures pinned proudly in frames on the wall.

Noah with Izzy.

Noah with Mikey.

Noah with her, Izzy and Mikey.

She stood a chance. She could do it.

For all of them.

Roman smacked her arse, letting it ripple, and pulled himself out, enjoying the sound of squelching. Two men's cum dribbled down her thigh and she resisted the need to vomit.

Then it occurred to her – if they thought he was finished, and he didn't leave the dining room, wouldn't they come looking for him?

She couldn't let Leon suspect anything.

So she started screaming again. Loudly. Imitating the moans and shrieks she had just been doing.

Roman looked at her, at first, confused. Then his face morphed into humour. He was intrigued.

She stood. Turned toward him. Displayed her naked body proudly.

She backed up, toward the cabinet, continuing making the noises, but making them more pleasurable, more enticing.

He edged toward her, smirking.

She ran her hands over her breasts. Over her belly. Over her clitoris. Over every part of her body, again and again, luring him in.

He rubbed his cock. Joined in with the noises, not realising just how stupid he was.

She reached the cabinet. Turned to face it. The dagger was behind the glass, inches from her eyes.

She stuck her arse out and said, "Do you think you could get hard again for me?"

He looked confused, suspicious. He was about to call her on it, thinking this was too strange, then she said, "I'm a little slut, remember? I love lots of cock…"

She slid her hand down her body, to her clitoris, where she touched herself, and her moans grew louder as her finger moved faster and faster.

"Yeah, all right," Roman said, "just give me a minute."

He turned away from her, and she watched him in the

reflection in the cabinet, staring down at his dick, trying with all his might to get it hard again.

He wouldn't manage. It didn't matter.

He was distracted.

She took the dagger out of the cabinet.

CHAPTER THIRTY-SEVEN

"That's strange," Leon said to Noah. "It sounded like he'd finished, but he's not come out. I thought he'd…"

Roman screamed.

"Ah, there he's off again!"

"Leon, please–"

"Shush, this is my favourite part!"

Roman kept screaming, and screaming again, his wails turning to shrieks.

"Wow, this is a big one…" Leon said. "Do you think they are going again? I mean, I'm always done after the first go, you know? But I know some guys like a second round…"

Noah was crying.

Leon could see Noah was crying.

He was surprised it had taken this long. He'd had tears from everyone else so far, and sobs from Noah, but only now was he really crying.

Leon shook his head. "Oh, Noah."

Noah looked down. Leon could see the opening plosive of the word *please* form on his lips, but the word did not come out. Noah had learnt by now that it did nothing. Begging only made it worse.

Leon relished the sight. Enjoyed every moment of it, and he enjoyed it even more as Noah's fists clenched and his body shook with rage, but he was too helpless to fight.

Instead, Noah looked at his son and the knife next to his throat, and Leon wondered just how far they could push this man.

Sooner or later, he would accept his family are going to die. All men do. Everyone has a breaking point, and you can tell a lot about a man as to how much prodding it takes to push him to it.

Michael Logan had a breaking point, but it had come much sooner than this. Leon hadn't even finished fucking Sylvia Logan before Michael snapped, and he tried to get up and attack Joanna.

It was at that point Leon had to kill Michael Logan's child. Michael and his wife had followed shortly after.

But Noah!

Oh, my, he was enduring. He was tougher, there was no doubt about it. This was going to be a longer night, which suited Leon, as he wanted to savour it.

Suddenly, Leon realised he was lost in thought, and that Roman was still screaming.

"Fuck," Leon said. "He's really going for it. Hope there's enough of the woman left for Declan."

"And her?" Noah said, pointing his head at Joanna. "What does she get? Does she get a turn?"

"If she wants, but I was more thinking she would be the one to kill her when Declan's done."

Noah tried to get up. In retrospect, Noah should have fought against them taking out his legs. If he'd known that they'd have hurt his family anyway, he would have at least thrown a few punches.

Then again, who was he kidding? He'd never thrown a punch in his life. Leon had grown up on the street. He'd have stood little chance.

But if Leon had grown up fighting, then Noah had grown up talking. He was a lawyer; it was his job to convince people of his point of view. So maybe he could try talking to Leon. Not his pathetic pleading, but real persuasion. Like he was giving the closing argument in a difficult case.

He took a deep breath, and figured he may as well try.

"You know, I am *not* Levi Isaacs," Noah said. "I am not the man who killed your brother. That is not me."

"But you defended him."

"I was doing my job."

"To get criminals off?"

"To ensure they got a fair trial! I wasn't trying to force a miscarriage of justice, I was simply trying to make sure my client's point of view was heard. Truth is, there was not enough evidence for a guilty verdict. I knew it, he knew it, even you probably knew it. Any other lawyer would have got the same result."

"Then that lawyer would have been the one listening to his wife being fucked, not you."

"Your brother was a criminal, Leon."

"What?"

"He dealt drugs. He mugged people. If he wasn't a criminal, do you think the police officer would have asked him what he was doing?"

"Think that makes a difference?"

"Yes. I'm sure Jamal was a good man in bad circumstances. We aren't all divided into honourable and evil people; we are all capable of good and bad things. But being poor didn't mean he deserved extra sympathy from the jury."

Leon leapt from his seat, strode toward Noah, and sent his fist flying into Noah's jaw, knocking him onto his front.

Noah pushed himself up and spat out a mouthful of blood.

"Doesn't mean the piggy should have killed him," Leon spat.

"Think it would have got to that if Jamal hadn't resisted arrest?"

"Breaking the law doesn't mean you deserve to die."

"What about me? I haven't broken the law, yet I deserve to die?"

Leon grabbed Noah by the hair and lifted his head up.

"My aunt is like you, you know. She grew up struggling like Ma did, then she married into money and stopped bothering with her. Money corrupts everything. Don't think you're the exception."

Roman stopped screaming.

"Ah, we're done." Leon dropped Noah. "Declan, get ready. It's time for her third course."

CHAPTER THIRTY-EIGHT

A ubrey's thighs sat either side of Roman's waist, her naked body dressed in robes of blood.

The multiple stab wounds in his chest and neck and face and arms were gushing with blood, and his face, that had only moments ago been screaming, was now still, and his eyes were staring up at her, empty and hollow.

She was panting.

Now she'd finished her frenzied attack, she could hear nothing but her own panting.

It wouldn't be long until they came looking for him. The next guy would come in to have his turn as soon as Roman left. They would be expecting Roman to walk out of that door within the next minute.

Which meant she had to hurry. She couldn't sit here and think about how she'd just killed a man.

But she had.

She'd just murdered him.

Oh, God, she'd just murdered him...

She'd stabbed him, and stabbed him again, and kept stabbing until his arms no longer fought and his body no longer squirmed.

She expected to feel guilty, or at least a little bad. She didn't. Her only thought was of her family.

She stood. Looked around.

She could creep out of the window behind her. It would take her to the back garden. From there, she could go around the front and find Izzy.

Though a part of her didn't want to see if Izzy was okay. She didn't want to see the body of her baby laying still and cold.

But she couldn't stay here. She'd come this far. Overpowered this man. Killed him. She had to move. Had to persevere.

She took off his jacket. Removed his trousers. They were stained in blood, but so was her body. She slipped them on and tightened the belt as much as she could. Zipped up the jacket. Placed the knife into the back of the belt. Crept along the room, her bare feet almost slipping on the growing puddle of blood.

She opened the window, and it creaked, so she stopped opening it and checked behind her.

No footsteps. No movement. Just the distant sound of Leon's voice gloating to her husband.

Oh, God, her husband. Her son.

They were both still in there.

First, Izzy.

Then the police.

Could she get to a neighbour and call them?

Would they kill her family and leave before she managed?

Stop deliberating.

This wasn't a time for overthinking. It was a time for action.

She reached her leg out of the window, her foot meeting the cold grass beneath the full moon, and climbed out.

She shut the window and crept through the garden, keeping low. Trying not to run. Not to be reckless. Despite the thudding of her heart and the tears on her cheeks and the blood on her hands. Despite every thought telling her to hurry, she could not mess this up.

She reached the side gate. Slipped the bolt across, slowly, silently. Crept past the front of the house.

When she reached the living room window, she lowered herself to her belly and crawled, not caring for the trails of mud left on her bloody clothes.

There she was.

Izzy.

Lying still on the hedge.

She crawled closer to her and cupped her baby's face.

Izzy's eyes were closed. She was unconscious.

But she was breathing.

She was actually breathing.

The bush must have cushioned her fall.

"Oh my God…" she whispered.

Izzy was alive.

CHAPTER THIRTY-NINE

Leon's foot tapped impatiently.

The silence had lasted far too long, and Noah was also feeling wary. He hated hearing his wife screaming, but at least he knew she was alive.

Leon looked at Declan, who was shifting nervously from one foot to the other. The others had looked eager and enthusiastic to enjoy Noah's wife; Declan didn't. He looked anxious. Like it was a first date.

Noah wondered how much Declan wanted to do all of this, and how much he had been coerced into it by his older brother.

"For fuck's sake…" Leon muttered.

He held Joanna's gaze for a moment. Both of them seemed agitated.

"Roman?" Leon called out, expecting an instant answer. Leon was evidently the man in charge of whatever they were doing, and he did not like to be made a fool of – not by Noah; not even by his friends.

Which was why he looked so angry when Roman didn't respond.

"Eh, Roman, what the fuck, man?"

Still nothing.

He looked at Joanna, huffed, and bit his lip.

"If he moves, cut the kid," he said, then charged through the room and through the dining room doors.

Noah was in immense amounts of physical pain, agonising mental turmoil, and felt emotionally destroyed – but, when he heard Leon scream, he couldn't help but gain a little bit of pride over his wife. He had no idea what she'd done, but she'd evidently done something.

"What the fuck!"

Leon's voice was loud, but with a sadness clinging to his words unlike Noah had witnessed so far. He could see from the look of Joanna's face that this was not normal. Leon did not normally show this kind of despair.

"Roman! Roman, come on!"

She wanted to go in and see what was happening, but she couldn't leave Noah and Mikey. For a moment, Noah considered whether this would be a good opportunity to fight back.

But how could he?

He tried pushing himself upwards, but his legs seized with pain.

"Roman, man, no! No!"

A few loud bangs made Noah jump. It sounded like Leon was punching the wall. It preceded the sound of the dining table being upturned and all of its contents smashing.

Noah peered through the crack in the door, and caught a glimpse of an arm next to a body. It was covered in blood.

Leon charged back in and stood, heaving, his face curled up, his body shaking with rage.

"What's going on?"

Leon didn't answer her.

His eyes met Noah's, and his nose curled into a snarl, and

before Noah could realise what was happening, Leon was on top of him, and he was lifting his arm back then sending his fist into Noah's face, over and over. It didn't bother Noah as much as it would have done a few hours ago. In a strange way, he'd become used to being in pain. His tolerance had increased, and whilst it hurt, and he tasted blood, it didn't stop him from gaining a bit of satisfaction from Leon's despair.

"Where is she?" Leon demanded.

Noah didn't answer.

"Where would she go?"

He looked up at Leon, blinking, feeling his cheeks begin to swell.

"Answer me! Where would she hide?"

Noah laughed. Leon punched him again.

"Answer me."

Leon leapt up and grabbed Mikey's throat.

Noah spat out a mouthful of blood and stayed on his back.

"She wouldn't hide," Noah said. "She's stronger than that."

"What are you talking about?"

"She'll have already called the police. You're fucked."

Leon and Joanna exchanged a look.

Leon let go of Mikey's neck and shoved him back toward Joanna.

"What's going on?" she asked. "Where's Roman?"

Leon's face curled up as he answered.

"Dead."

"What?"

"She killed him."

Leon looked at Declan, who gazed back with a vulnerability so unlike the others.

"What you going to do?" Joanna asked.

Leon didn't answer. The look he gave her was enough.

In a strange act of affection, he gave her a kiss, a passionate one, then pulled away. She looked up at him like he was her messiah. Like she worshipped him.

He flexed his fingers over his knife.

"They try anything, kill the boy."

He charged to the front door, opened it, and left.

CHAPTER FORTY

Aubrey didn't have much time to be grateful for small miracles.

Izzy was alive, but she wasn't conscious, and the front door was opening, and Leon was stepping outside. Shadows concealed her, but not for long.

Izzy needed an ambulance. They needed the police. She needed to get across the lawn, across the driveway, and run down the road to the nearest neighbour – but as soon as Leon appeared in the moonlight, she felt her hope quickly dissipate.

He stomped up the driveway, then stopped at the gate, searching for her down the street.

He was blocking her route.

She looked for another way. It was no good. The fences surrounding the front garden were too high. She could scream, but the neighbours were too far away, and Leon would find her before they even began to wonder what that noise in the distance was.

So what next?

If she couldn't run, she could hide. Try to find a way to contact the outside.

Their phones weren't working. The router wire had been cut. Even so, she was sure there was a spare router somewhere.

But how was she meant to setup a new router without being caught?

Leon marched to the end of the driveway and peered up and down the street, but he didn't leave. The gate was still locked. If he hadn't realised that she hadn't left the property yet, he soon would.

And he looked angry. Fuming. His body was hunched over. His fists clenched. His footsteps heavy.

He must have found Roman.

She looked down at Roman's clothes. Too big for her and covered in his blood. This would infuriate Leon even more. He'd think she was mocking him.

She cradled Izzy and stroked her hair. She may be alive now, but she wasn't waking up and she wasn't crying and Aubrey worried just how long she was going to last.

What would give her daughter the best chance of survival?

Warmth, she decided. It was too cold. She had to put Izzy somewhere inside.

Leon searched the bushes that lined the fences.

Aubrey took a deep breath, refused to think about how Izzy was probably beyond saving, and crept through the shadows at the front of the house.

She paused by the front door, knowing the porch light would illuminate her, and looked at Leon.

He was still searching the bushes. He had his back to her.

Izzy made a sound. A small one. A quiet moan that, minutes earlier, would have made Aubrey so happy. Now, however, it caught Leon's attention, and he spun around.

Aubrey retreated into the shadow and crouched beside a bush, making herself as small as she could, and held her breath.

As Leon scanned the front of the house, his eyes passed her a few times.

He stepped toward the house.

"Aubrey?" he said.

Aubrey's lips pressed firmly together.

"Oh, Aubrey, I know you're there. And I know Izzy is too."

Her forehead rested against Izzy, her face scrunched up, shutting out all sounds.

"By now you know it's too late for you... But if you let me know where you are, I'll think about sparing Izzy."

Leon stopped, poked the bush just across from her, giving it a kick, then taking a few steps and rustling the bush again.

It was a matter of seconds. He was going to find her. She knew it.

She had to act.

She had to do something.

Leon kicked the bush again, then stepped closer. She could smell his sweat. It was the same smell from when he...

She shook herself out of it.

Now was not the time.

"Aubrey..."

She held Izzy tight to her chest, breathed calmly and silently, in through the nose, out through the mouth.

She could use the knife. Noah's ceremonial dagger was in the back of the belt. She could stick it into Leon's neck the moment he found her.

But what if she missed?

What if he blocked it?

Leon was street-smart. A fighter. He'd see it coming. Even with a weapon, he'd probably beat her.

So she made her decision.

She was going to run.

She was going to get back into the house and find somewhere warm to hide Izzy.

Then she'd figure out the next part.

Leon stepped toward her and, just as he went to kick the bush and grab her from her hiding place, she leapt forward, barged him out of the way, and sprinted to the gate that returned her to the back garden.

CHAPTER FORTY-ONE

The ceiling spun.

Noah had never really looked at it before.

Strange, really, how you can buy a house, live in it every day, and not know what the ceiling looked like. Until today, he would not be able to say what colour it was. Now, laying upon his back on the thick carpet of the living room, he realised how repulsed he was by its sickly cream colour.

He turned his head to the side. Looked at Mikey, who stared back. His cheeks were red with glistening tears, and the urine on his pyjamas was now dry. He was shaking. It was cold. Even if it wasn't, Joanna had been holding her blade close to Mikey's throat for a long time now, and Mikey must be terrified.

Although it was starting to lose its impact on Noah.

What a bizarre thought...

The sight of a knife against his son's throat, the constant pain in his legs, and the knowledge that his wife and daughter may be dead – these were things that one does not easily get used to.

Yet, at this point, he had.

The constant threat had become his life now. It was still frightening, but it was not something new.

And, as he realised that he was becoming numb to constant fear, he hated himself for it.

"Hey, Champ?" he said, ignoring Joanna's glare.

Mikey's eyes widened. Noah tried to offer him a smile.

"How's it going?"

"Shut up!" Joanna snapped. "No talking."

Noah ignored her.

"Hang in there," Noah said. "It'll be over soon. Okay?"

Mikey nodded.

What a smart kid. A strong boy. Noah had raised him well.

Noah shifted his stare to Joanna.

"He your husband?" Noah asked.

"What?" Joanna barked.

"Leon. He your husband?"

"He's my boyfriend."

"Ah. And this is the kind of stuff you like to do together, is it?"

"I thought I told you to shut up."

"Cause anarchy? Have your vengeance?"

"You want to see your son die?"

"Did you mind Leon having sex with another woman?"

Joanna's nose curled. Her lip raised. She was angry, and Noah was enjoying it.

"Just figured, since he went into the other room and had sex with another woman…"

My wife, he wanted to say. *He had sex with my wife.*

But he couldn't bring himself to say it.

"He just cheated on you, didn't he?"

"It's not cheating."

"You in an open relationship or something? You polyamorous?"

"No, it just wasn't about sex."

"Ah, right. What was it about then?"

"Vengeance."

Noah thought about this for a moment, then let out a laugh, and watched Joanna's eyes widen into fury as he did.

"So let me get this straight – you let him have sex with another woman because he tells you it's about vengeance, not about sex."

"It isn't about sex."

"You are bloody gullible."

"Just one more word and I'll–"

"What about you?" Noah turned to Declan, stood in the corner, shifting his body weight from one foot to the other.

Joanna gave him an *I'm warning you* look, but Noah could see that Declan was the weak link. He looked nervous all the time. Whilst the others committed atrocities with smiles on their faces, Declan was shaking, his arms wrapped around himself, his eyes shooting around the room, looking at anything but a person.

"You don't want to do this, do you?" Noah asked.

"You don't talk to him," Joanna said.

Noah ignored her.

"You could help us, you know."

"I said leave him alone."

"I can tell you know this is wrong. You're not like the others, are you?"

"Declan, get over here."

Declan looked nervously at Joanna.

"I said get over here."

He shuffled past Noah, to Joanna.

"Wait in the hallway," she told him, and he stepped out of the room and into the downstairs hallway.

Joanna turned back to Noah.

"You think you're being clever, don't you?" she said.

"You really want to know what I think? I think you can't kill either of us without Leon's permission."

"You think that do you?"

"Yes. You keep threatening it, but you don't do it."

He told himself to stop talking. What was he doing? His taunts may throw her off, but for what? He couldn't get up and fight. He was only going to make her more unstable.

"Do you want to see if I'm willing to kill your son?" she asked.

Noah didn't reply.

"Go on. Tease me some more. Say yes, I want to know, Joanna. Say it, and we'll see what I'm willing to do. We'll see whether I need Leon's permission."

Noah looked into the eyes of his son, who was crying again.

"Go on. Say it. I dare you."

Noah said nothing.

CHAPTER FORTY-TWO

Aubrey clung onto Izzy with all she had and fled Leon's grasp. She ran, and he chased her, his footsteps loud stomps behind her.

She considered whether she could make it across the driveway and away from the house, but she didn't have the keys for the gate and he'd grab her before she climbed over it, so she sprinted around the side of the house instead.

She just managed to unbolt the garden gate as his hand reached her arm, but she stepped out of his clutches before he could clamp his fingers around her wrist and slammed the garden gate in his face, even managing to bolt it.

She knew it wouldn't delay him for long. In fact, she'd only managed a few steps before he'd kicked the gate open and entered the garden.

There was a wooden trellis panel against the house that ended by Izzy's room. The window was open; that must have been how Joanna and Declan had entered the house. Could she climb up it?

If she fell, it could kill Izzy.

But she had no time to think.

No time to doubt herself.

Need to move. Just ignore the thoughts and move.

She approached the trellis and, ignoring the thorns wrapped around the wood, she placed her fingers through the first panel. With her other arm wrapped around Izzy, she placed her feet into another panel and climbed upwards just as Leon made it into the garden.

His fingers grabbed Roman's bloody trousers, but her petite stature made her far nimbler than he, and she made it halfway up the trellis and out of reach. By the time he'd started climbing, she was at the window. She placed a foot on the ledge and then, without giving it any thought, hurled herself in, landing on her back, clutching Izzy to her chest.

Izzy's wooden mobile rotated above her cot, and the pictures of farm animals Noah had painted on the walls glared back at her.

She rushed to the wardrobe. Opened the doors. Placed Izzy on the floor, on some clothes, and covered her body with a few jackets, creating a makeshift bed.

That's when Izzy opened her eyes.

She was conscious.

Aubrey was ecstatic, then terrified. Her child was coming around, which meant she was okay – but did this mean she was going to cry?

"Shush, Izzy, please, just be quiet," Aubrey whispered, trying to keep her voice calm rather than frantic. She wasn't successful.

She looked over her shoulder. Leon's grunts grew louder.

"Please, go back to sleep."

Izzy's eyes closed again, and her head tilted to the side, and she went back to sleep.

Finally. A little bit of luck.

She closed the wardrobe and rushed across the room, just as Leon fell in with a large thud.

He looked up at her as she ran out of the room and fled into the hallway.

But he didn't go after her.

Why didn't he go after her?

She stopped. Turned back. He dragged the cot across the room, grinned at her, and shut the door to the bedroom.

Izzy...

Aubrey rushed to the door and tried to open it.

It was no good. He'd blocked it.

Izzy...

What was he doing?

What was he going to do to her baby?

Izzy...

She shouldn't have been so stupid.

How did she think that would be a good idea?

Leaving her baby hidden in there...

She charged at the door. Again and again. And again. And again.

It didn't buckle.

She stood back. What was she going to do?

Voices came from downstairs. Noah. Joanna. Talking.

Her eyes narrowed. Her arms tensed. She was sick of these people tormenting her family.

She was going to get some collateral. Something she could threaten Leon with. Something she could use to get Izzy back.

She took the dagger from her belt and ran downstairs.

CHAPTER FORTY-THREE

A stumble and a clatter made them turn toward the stairs, just visible in the hallway through the open living room door.

Joanna, with concern.

Declan, without a clue.

Noah, with hope.

He looked at Mikey. He wanted to say, *that's your mum, I know it is, she's going to help us.*

But he daren't.

He glanced at Joanna, who clutched Mikey a little harder.

And at Declan, who stood behind her in the hallway, pacing back and forth then walking in circles.

And then came the most glorious sight from behind Joanna: Aubrey, rushing down the steps two at a time, wearing Roman's jacket, covered in his blood, with the ceremonial dagger she had complained about only the other day.

She held the dagger above her head with both hands, looked into Declan's wide eyes, and plunged the blade into his throat as she took him to the floor.

She screamed, her voice growing hoarse, as she retracted

the knife and brought it down on his throat again, then lifted the knife and brought it down again.

Declan gargled, his eyes full of terror; you could see in those eyes the realisation that he was about to die, a mixture of suffocation and realisation. He was grabbing his throat, blood rushing between his fingers, his legs kicking, wriggling back and forth until, eventually, his body lay still.

His leg throbbed, as did his arm, but his wide eyes no longer moved, and the arms that were clutching his neck fell.

Aubrey, her hair mixed with blood, her face painted in red, turned to Joanna.

The sight of his wife scared Noah.

He was grateful for her fighting; she'd cut the number of their assailants in half. But, if he'd been asked whether Aubrey was capable of killing two men before today, the answer would have been an unequivocal, resounding no.

Yet here she was.

Joanna went to respond, but dawdled too long, taken aback, leaving herself open for Aubrey to dive on her, taking her away from Mikey and onto the floor.

Joanna, however, did not go down as easily as Declan. Aubrey mounted her opponent, lifted the knife into the air, and plunged it downwards, only to be blocked by Joanna's arm.

Noah opened his arms and beckoned Mikey toward him. Mikey ran into his dad's embrace, wrapping his arms tightly around him, and crying into his shoulder.

"I know," Noah said. "I know. It's okay. It's going to be okay."

Noah took another look at Aubrey and Joanna, wrestling on the floor. Whatever was powering Aubrey, whether it be adrenaline or fury, was working. Joanna was beneath her, resisting her attacks, and whilst she was blocking each of

Aubrey's strikes, it was still clear that Aubrey was the one on top.

Noah held Mikey in front of him, gripping his arms, looking him in the eyes as calmly as he could. He had to show strength to Mikey, a boy who had already experienced more trauma than any person should.

"Listen to me," Noah said. "This is not over yet. Understand? This is not over."

"What? Please make them go…"

"I know, Mikey, I know. We're trying. But for now, you need to leave us grown-ups to it, yeah? You need to leave us to fight off the bad guys, and you need to go hide."

"But why can't you come with me?"

Noah looked down at his legs. He wasn't going anywhere.

"I can't. I'm too badly injured."

"I don't want to go anywhere where–"

"I will come find you. When this is over, I will come find you, I promise. But for now, you need to think of the best hiding place you can, and I need you to stay there and make absolutely no sound. You understand? No sound at all."

"But I don't want to."

"I know you don't, but I need you to, do you understand me? Mikey, please, I need you to."

Noah tried to quell his tears as he stared into his son's eyes, seeing how lost he looked, seeing how scared he was, how he did not want to be separated from his parents again. But Noah also knew he was a strong child. The kind who stood up to bullies. The kind who had the confidence to tell a teacher when they had an answer wrong. The kind who believed that his parents knew best.

"I love you," Noah said. "Now be brave and go. Go!"

Mikey cried. Noah did what he hated to do, and pushed him away, and Mikey turned and ran upstairs.

Within seconds, he was gone.

Noah turned to the scuffle between Aubrey and Joanna, and tried pulling himself along the floor by his hands, hoping he could help.

"Leon!" Joanna screamed, so loud it strained her voice, just as she blocked yet another strike.

Aubrey looked possessed. Lifting the dagger and lunging it down, over and over, aiming for Joanna's neck, trying and trying despite being constantly blocked.

Noah dragged himself along the carpet. They were at the other side of the room, but all he could do was drag himself slowly across the floor, until he finally reached their side and grabbed Joanna's arms. She tried to free herself from his grasp, but he held tightly, pulling her arms out of the way.

"Do it," he told Aubrey.

She lifted the dagger high into the air.

Aimed at the throat.

Lunged it downwards – then halted.

Just before the blade met the skin, she stopped.

Not because she didn't want to, nor because she didn't have the guts or because she didn't see Joanna as anything but a monster.

She stopped for the same reason that Noah loosened his grip and let Joanna's arms go.

Because they heard the sound of a crying baby coming down the stairs.

CHAPTER FORTY-FOUR

L eon walked down the stairs casually, like it was a Sunday morning and he could smell breakfast, cradling their crying baby.

Noah and Aubrey both froze. Noah at Joanna's side, Aubrey mounting her, but with her knife in the air; she would not move another inch for fear of Izzy's life.

For fear of what Leon would do to Izzy after seeing his dead brother.

Leon didn't move. He stood by Declan's side, looking down at the corpse. His face looked stern, but Noah could see the cracks in the façade. He could see the anger, the hostility pushing at the surface, his attempt to keep his expression blank; his desperation to retain control.

No one said anything for quite a while.

Everyone waited on Leon's next move, nothing but the wails of their aggravated daughter filling the silence.

Without removing his stare from Declan, Leon spoke.

"Get off of her," he stated, cold, emotionless.

Aubrey slowly and cautiously stood up and stepped to the side, away from Joanna.

Joanna stood, brushing herself off and straightening her top. After a quick glance at Aubrey, she swung her fist into the face of the woman who so nearly killed her, prompting flickers of blood to spray over Joanna's face.

She didn't even blink.

"Take the knife," Leon stated, still with his focus on his brother.

Aubrey hesitated.

Noah pleaded with her in his mind not to give up her only weapon, her only leverage. But Aubrey wasn't looking at him. She was staring at Izzy, with the look of a desperate mother.

She gave Joanna the knife, who placed her fingers tight around the handle, and held it up to the light.

"Holy shit," she said. "This is one hell of a fucking knife. What is it?"

She looked to Aubrey, then to Noah.

"Eh, what is it?"

Noah paused, then said, "It's a ceremonial dagger."

"Fuck me. It's beautiful. Is this what you killed Roman with too?"

Aubrey didn't want to answer.

"Eh?"

Finally, she gave a faint nod.

Leon knelt at the feet of his brother, then placed Izzy carefully beside him. He watched how one stayed still, whilst the other fidgeted and fussed and cried.

"Six months ago," he said. "I had two brothers."

He looked at Noah.

"Now I'm an only child."

He turned to Aubrey.

"I should strangle your baby."

"No!" she cried out, and Joanna held her back.

"I should throttle her until the crying stops. I should desecrate her remains, then shit all over your corpse too."

159

"You brought this fight to us," Noah said, unable to help himself.

"You what?"

Leon's eyebrows narrowed, his eyes leered, his face turned red. Noah knew he'd said something he shouldn't have. But he also knew that, should he say nothing, Leon would kill him anyway.

He was a good lawyer. He could talk himself out of any situation. He'd managed to get Levi Isaacs off, after all. He would continue trying to fight with words.

"You get angry with us for killing your brother, and your friend, but we wouldn't have done if you'd never interfered with our lives."

"If *I* hadn't interfered with *your* lives?"

"Yes. Had you just left us alone, this would never have happened."

"No – if you had never defended a *murderer*, this would never have happened."

"You have no idea about hard work. You just prove everyone right. That you're all just criminals."

"Oh, is that what we are, is it?"

Leon stood, sticking his bottom lip out and nodding sarcastically. Noah could see Leon's rage intensifying.

"You think because you sit here in your big house doing your big job, that you're better than me?"

"Not better. Just different."

"No, I think you mean *better*."

Noah knew he was making things worse. But he knew he could make it better. It was like investing in stocks – you had to be prepared to make a loss to ultimately make a win.

"I think we come from very different walks of life, and perhaps we wouldn't interact because of that reason. Not because of how much is in your wallet."

"Noah, shut up," Aubrey interjected, her eyes closed and her head turned away.

"Nah, please. Let the man speak. I imagine you're going to start talking next about how you can help me. Put me in a program. Help find me a better life."

"I could, if that's what you wanted."

"And what's wrong with my life as it is now?"

"You're doing bad things. They are wrong."

"Nah, I'm doing illegal things, not bad things."

"What's the difference?"

"What you did was legal. But it was still bad."

"For Christ's sake, Noah," Aubrey said. "You're making it worse."

"Your bitch is right," Leon said. "All you've done is show me exactly why we're doing this."

Leon looked over his shoulder at his brother, and Izzy lying beside him. She had finally stopped crying, but her eyes were still open and she still wriggled.

"You know what," Leon said. "I warned you, didn't I? I warned you over and over, you fuck about with me, we kill your family. Didn't I?"

"I don't think you want to do that."

"Don't you?"

"No. And I don't think you will."

Leon turned to Joanna.

"It's over to you, my love," he said.

Joanna nodded. Turned to Aubrey. Grinned, then stuck the dagger into her belly. She even gave Aubrey a delicate kiss before letting her body slide off the dagger and drop limply on the floor.

Noah screamed like he was in hell itself.

CHAPTER FORTY-FIVE

Where was the best hiding place?

There was his toy chest, if Mikey could get all the toys out, but then they might see all the toys and he might not have time and they might find him.

There was under the bed, but he didn't like it under the bed, he always thought there were monsters there which was a crazy thought when the real monsters are downstairs.

Under his duvet?

Don't be silly, Mikey.

Dad said he needed to be grown up. Dad said he needed to be brave, right after Dad had said that he loved him.

And they would see him under the duvet.

He could lock himself in the bathroom.

But they'd know where he was, and they might barge the door open, and then he would be trapped.

He rushed from his room, to the bathroom, to the guest bedroom, where the bed was always made and the cupboard drawers were always empty.

There was nowhere in here.

Think, Mikey, think.

Shouting. Coming from downstairs. Dad was screaming. Really loudly.

Why was he screaming?

Mikey had never heard Dad scream. He'd never seen him afraid, or scared, or worried, or anything. Dad was always… Dad. Thoughtful and calm.

And now he was screaming.

And Mikey needed to find a place to hide, quickly.

He rushed from the guest bedroom to his parent's bedroom. He knew he wasn't supposed to be in here, and that Mum and Dad always told him that he needed to stay out, but he was sure they wouldn't mind if he could find a good hiding place.

They had a bed he could hide under too.

Stop being stupid, Mikey. You can't hide under a bed. They will find you there.

But where could he go where he couldn't be found?

He opened Mum and Dad's cupboard. There could be enough space for him in there.

What about Izzy's bedroom? Under her cot maybe…

But they could still find him there.

What about Mum?

Would she be okay?

What had she done to that strange man?

He'd seen Mum cry before. He'd seen her shout at Dad and he'd seen her get upset and he'd seen her in a strop. But he'd never seen her angry and attacking someone like he had.

Stop it, Mikey.

You're being silly again.

Dad said you have to be brave, so be brave. Be like a knight in one of the stories. Or an Avenger. Or a jedi.

What would a jedi do?

They would fight. They would use their mind control or their lightsabres and they would defeat everyone.

You're not a jedi, Mikey.

You're a child.

Just hide.

He ran back out of the room, across the landing, trying to keep his footsteps light, trying not to be scared, desperate to find a decent hiding place.

But he couldn't.

There was nowhere to hide where they wouldn't find him.

He caught sight of the strange man covered in blood lying on the floor downstairs. Izzy was next to him. Lying there. Her body wriggling.

He ran back to his room.

Back to the bathroom.

To the guest bedroom.

To Mum and Dad's bedroom.

There was no good place.

But he had to find somewhere.

He had to.

And he had to hurry.

Finally, he settled on a place. It would keep him safe for now. They could find him there, but it didn't matter, he just had to stay there, stay still, and wait for Mum and Dad.

They'd come get him when they were ready.

When the bad people had gone.

They would.

He was sure of it.

CHAPTER FORTY-SIX

"**N**o!"

The echoes of Noah's scream died out. He couldn't move. Not just because of his wounded legs, but because of the sight before him.

Aubrey.

Laid on her back.

He had no idea how long he was staring at her, time no longer existed, but he was still staring at her long after she'd stopped moving.

In fact, he couldn't remember when she'd stopped moving, but she had.

Blood flowed out of her, the puddle expanding, spreading beneath the armchair they'd bought together a few years ago. They'd both agreed on the same armchair. They'd laughed about it. It was probably the only item they'd ever agreed on. They'd said it was a miracle.

A *miracle.*

Noah dropped his head. Closed his eyes. He couldn't look anymore.

Fingers pressed into the sides of his skull. Hands lifted his head and a low, sinister voice said in his ear, "Look at her."

He refused.

"Look at her!"

He obeyed. Opened his eyes. Looked at the still, empty body of his wife.

"You thought they were just threats, didn't you?"

Yes, he had.

Not at first, not when they first arrived, but they'd said so many times that they were going to kill his family that the words had begun to lose meaning.

Now they had followed through on their promise.

Now they had killed…

He dropped his head. Closed his eyes. He couldn't even think it.

Leon lifted his head again.

"I said look at her."

Noah pulled his head out of Leon's grip and turned to him, scowling, his lips curling with the rage he could no longer deny. His arms were twitching, he was panting, he was shaking.

Leon stood back and marvelled at what they had created.

"You feel that?" Leon said. "Right now, you feel what that is, coursing through you?"

Noah tried pushing himself to his feet, but the agony in his legs forced a scream and he fell back down. He was unable to use his rage, unable to fight, unable to do anything. His wife's body lay next to him, and he could do nothing but glare at the man and woman responsible.

"You feel it, don't you? I know you do."

Leon exchanged a smile with Joanna, who was wiping Aubrey's blood off the dagger and onto her jeans.

"That feeling. It's anger." Leon crouched down to Noah's level. "It's fury. It's vengeance. It is everything I felt when my brother was killed. It's also justice – the kind that you took from me."

Noah turned away.

He couldn't hear any more of it.

But, as he turned his head away, he saw Aubrey.

And he couldn't look at her either.

In fact, he couldn't do anything.

If he thought, he thought of Aubrey. If he looked, he looked at her or her murderers. If he closed his eyes, he just saw the look on her face as Joanna put the dagger in Aubrey's belly and she realised that death was imminent.

It hurt him to see that face.

He wanted to protect her. Not that he'd ever needed to, she was a strong woman who'd never needed him to stand up for her – but it hurt him to see even a flicker of pain.

It was all his fault.

They were here because of him.

And now she was dead because of him.

"Just kill me," Noah said. "Just do it. Put me out of my misery."

"Finally, Noah. You've reached that point. It took Michael Logan only an hour to reach it – you've done much better."

Leon looked at Aubrey's body.

"Shame, really," he said. "She was a beautiful woman. And a great fuck, too. Wouldn't you say?"

Noah didn't meet Leon's eyes. He felt sick. He turned the other way, wanting to scream, wanting to cry, but being unable to do anything but throw up blood and bile, all over the carpet.

The carpet he and Aubrey had picked together when they'd bought this house.

"Michael Logan puked too," Leon said. "Again, it took you longer."

"Just kill me. Just end it. I've had enough."

"Almost, Noah. Almost."

"Almost?" Noah's voice buckled under the volume of his words. "What else do you want to do to me? What else could you possibly do to me?"

"There is one more thing you have to witness, then it's over, Noah. I promise."

Noah dropped his head. Closed his eyes. He was tired and drowsy, and he was tempted to give into it, but what Leon said next made him resist.

"Go find his son," Leon told Joanna. "It's time to end this."

CHAPTER FORTY-SEVEN

Joanna took the stairs quietly, rotating the dagger in her hand. It was so much better than her knife, and she was grateful to Aubrey for giving it to her.

She paused at the top step.

Looked back and forth. Listened.

Oh, how she enjoyed this part. It was like a game of hide and seek, only with dire consequences. Instead of *I found you, now it's my turn to hide*, the stakes were more *I found you, now it's your turn to die.*

She used to play this game as a child. Not with any siblings, as she had none. Nor with her parents, who wouldn't have given enough of a shit about her to play any kind of game that didn't involve drinking or assault. No, she would play it with the cat. But the cat would always win. She would never be able to find it.

Until the day she did, when she'd dragged the old, rusty can-opener across its belly and listened to the sounds it made as it slowly died.

"Mikey…" she called out playfully. "Oh, Mikey, where are you?"

Honestly, she liked this kid. He was far more interesting than Michael Logan's kid, who had been a right weirdo, and had kept asking her stupid questions – *why won't Mommy move? Why is Daddy screaming? Why are you carrying a knife?* He was an imbecile, that kid. And he looked weird, with big ears and a weird stare. Mikey was a handsome boy, at least. Not a bad kid to look at. He'd be a right stunner when he's older.

Well, he would have been.

She turned to her right and started with the far bedroom. Mikey's bedroom. The place where they had met only a few hours ago, and the most likely place an idiot would hide.

"Oh, Mikey, Mikey… Come out, come out, wherever you are…"

She dragged his duvet back with the knife, knowing that he wasn't there but wanting to be thorough. She went to her hands and knees and looked under the bed. Wandered to the curtains and looked behind them. Then she checked the only remaining place of concealment in the room; his wardrobe.

Nothing.

Though the kid had a lot of clothes.

Then again, his parents could afford them, couldn't they? Joanna had been lucky if her parents had brought some raggedy shit from Oxfam. Most of what she had she'd stolen herself.

She left the bedroom, re-entered the hallway, and paused outside the bathroom. The door was closed. Had he locked himself in?

Was that really his best hiding place?

"Oh, Mikey…"

She turned the handle and the door opened without a problem. Perhaps he wasn't so stupid.

She checked behind the shower curtain. Checked behind the door.

Empty.

She returned to the hallway. There were three bedrooms left. First, the guest bedroom.

"Mikey, Mikey, are you in here…"

The bed was made but, just to be sure, she stuck the dagger in the middle of it, only to penetrate nothing but mattress.

She checked under the bed. Clear.

In the wardrobe. Nothing.

Then she went to Izzy's bedroom and searched under the cot, in the wardrobe, behind the stuffed toys. There was nothing.

Which left one more bedroom.

Her smile widened. She entered the room and closed the door behind her, pausing at the entrance, looking around.

"Mikey… I know you're in here…"

She scanned the room, looking for the most likely places.

"Mikey, you know I'm going to find you…"

She lifted back the duvet.

Checked under the bed.

Checked under the dresser.

Looked out of the open window, into the garden. He could have climbed out, of course. The little shit could be running away and getting help right that very moment.

Then the sound of stifled breath took her away from the thought.

It was faint, but it was definite. She'd heard it.

"Oh, Mikey, come on… Let's not be silly, now…"

The only place left was the wardrobe.

She stayed completely still, listening carefully.

His breathing was heavy.

She knew where he was.

With the dagger at her side, she approached.

CHAPTER FORTY-EIGHT

The room spun. Noah lay on his back, thoughts firing, considering what he could do.

He had to protect Mikey.

He had to protect Izzy.

And Aubrey…

He had to stop thinking about her. Put her out of his mind. Put his *dead wife* out of his mind.

Oh God… They'd stabbed her…

Stop it. Your children need you.

Aubrey would want you to protect your children.

But how? He couldn't even stand, let alone get to his knees. There was no way.

But there had to be.

But there wasn't.

Stop thinking stupid thoughts.

But what other thoughts could he think? Any thought of retaliation was a stupid one. If it was just him left, he'd probably just let them kill him.

But his baby lay next to Declan's corpse, and that psychotic woman was upstairs searching for his son.

What was he supposed to do?

Whatever it was, he had to do it. He had to put up some kind of fight. However pathetic, he had to let go of what Leon had done to his legs and use his arms, or whatever he had.

"You should see your face right now," Leon said, sat next to Aubrey's body.

Noah turned away. He couldn't look at her.

"Shit, your thoughts must be racing."

He wished Leon would shut up. All night he'd heard him talking and talking, and his voice was starting to grate. It was non-stop, all the time, just one taunt after another.

"After all, you've seen what we can do to your wife, and now—"

"Would you shut up?"

Noah hadn't meant to say it, but it came out. Even so, he didn't regret it.

"You what?"

"Just please, shut up. All the time with your talking, it's incessant. I'd take my battered legs over listening to you whine on and on all night."

Leon raised his eyebrows.

"I mean, one minute it's 'oh, I'm going to kill your family,' the next it's 'oh, you're such an arsehole, Noah,' then it's like, 'oh, my brother, he's dead, wah wah bloody wah.' I mean, let's be straight, your brother was a dick."

"My brother was a good man."

"He was a piece of shit. I'm not saying that the police officer should have done what he did, but the world isn't going to cry over losing another criminal."

Leon stood. Straightened his jacket, smoothed down his sleeves. Walked over to Noah.

"And what you don't seem to get, as well, is just because he's poor, doesn't mean he can't be a prick. It isn't just rich people who do stupid shit, you know?"

Leon stomped on Noah's head, smacking it against the floor. For a moment, Noah's vision lacked focus, and a head rush disorientated him, then he was okay again.

He knew he was onto something.

He pushed himself up, resting on his hands, turning to Leon's legs.

Leon's legs.

His legs…

If Noah could take out Leon's legs, then it would be a fair fight.

"What I did in defending Levi Isaacs was wrong."

He looked up at Leon, at that menacing sneer, knowing he just needed to push him a little more, force his guard to drop.

"It was wrong, but I don't regret it."

Leon kicked Noah in the chin, forcing him onto his back. He pushed himself up again, resting on his hands.

"One more police officer on the street beating criminals to death isn't going to bother me."

Leon kicked Noah again, this time impacting his cheek bone.

Noah rolled onto his back, feeling his face throb, then pushed himself back to his hands.

And he looked at his wife.

And he saw something – something he wasn't entirely sure he'd seen. He was dizzy, his mind could be playing tricks on him.

Then he saw it again.

Her hand. It twitched. A small, slight movement.

But he was sure he'd seen it.

She was alive. She had to be.

"I hope that, once you get caught for this," Noah said, with renewed vigour, "some rich bastard kills you too."

Leon lifted his leg back, getting as much momentum as he could, and swung it at Noah.

Noah, however, caught it. And, in the instant his hands wrapped around Leon's ankle, he sunk his teeth into Leon's calf, biting harder and harder until blood dribbled down his chin.

Leon tried shaking his leg free, but Noah refused to let go.

CHAPTER FORTY-NINE

"Oh Mikey, come on, let's not be silly now…"

Mikey knew his breathing was too loud, that she could probably hear him, that she was probably walking toward the wardrobe at that very moment, so he held it, hoping that she wouldn't know he was there.

But he could hear her. Her footsteps were heavy, and they were coming closer.

Which meant he was going to have to run.

As soon as she opened the door, he would run.

Her footsteps paused. He could hear her breathing outside the door; he could even hear a little chuckle.

"Mikey, I am giving you the chance to come out yourself. We don't need any of this nonsense now, do we?"

Mikey closed his eyes. Readied himself.

Dad said be brave.

So he'd be brave.

She swung the door open.

"Gotcha!"

He let his breath go and ran, only for Joanna to grab his

collar. She had a hold of him, and he could see the dagger in her hand, and it was covered in blood, and Dad said to be brave, so be brave, Mikey, *be brave.*

He flailed his arms, intending to hit her but with no idea whether he did, he just threw them in every direction, catching a nose, and an eye, and a chin, until she was forced to drop him.

He ran again, then her foot met his ankle and he fell flat on his face.

She grabbed him by the hair and hoisted him to his feet.

He stared up at her. She looked like she should be pretty, but she wasn't. There was too much about her facial expression that wasn't right. The way she looked at him, the way she smiled, it was all... *wrong.*

"I'm starting to like you, kid," she said. "Don't piss me off."

Mikey struggled, thrashed his arms again, hitting and fighting her.

Her smile quickly faded. His retaliation was nothing but a minor inconvenience. She grabbed his collar and dragged him forward, driving his head into the wall beside the open window.

"I will knock you the fuck out," she told him. "Now knock it off."

But he didn't knock it off.

As soon as she went to pick him up again, he fought and fought and thrashed and thrashed and she had to hit his head against the wall a second time.

He was dizzy, but he was being brave, so he continued to fight, and fight, and she tried to hit him into the wall a third time – except, this time he put all his weight to his side, and he missed the wall, and he ended up falling out of the window instead.

Mikey could tell she didn't mean to do that, because he

heard her go, "Aw, shit," just as he fell – but then he was falling and he wasn't thinking about her.

He landed in a bush. The thorns hurt his back, sticking into his skin, but it didn't hurt anywhere near as much as being thrown into a wall.

Joanna's face appeared out of the window, and Mikey knew, even at such a young age, that this was his opportunity, his chance to run.

So he took it.

He ran away from the bush, picking bits of twig off his skin, and sprinted to the garden gate, which he unbolted and opened, and continued to sprint across the front lawn and the driveway.

He reached the gate, but it was locked. He peered down the road from between the bars. All the houses were so far away. But he saw a car. Coming toward them. In the distance. Its headlights shining.

He just had to get their attention.

He waved his hands, shouted, but they were driving slowly and he wished they'd hurry up. Dad was always complaining about the speed bumps and how annoying they were, and Mum was always saying how they were necessary – how those speed bumps kept people below twenty miles per hour.

There were footsteps behind him. The car was taking too long.

He waved his arms, hoping to get their attention, and the headlights grew brighter, and they grew closer, and then–

And then he felt a hand around his mouth and an arm around his chest, and was brought back onto the driveway.

The headlights went past and didn't stop.

Mikey tried to shout, but his voice was muffled by her hand. He bit her finger and she instinctively pulled it away.

Mikey tried to shout again, but Joanna grabbed the back of

his hair, pushed him to the ground, and hit his head into the concrete. He felt dizzy, and she did it again, and he saw a droplet of blood.

She forced him to his feet. He was too disorientated to fight back, and she was able to drag him back into the house.

CHAPTER FIFTY

Leon shook his leg like it was on fire, but Noah held on, his arms wrapped around Leon's ankle, and his teeth dug into Leon's calf. Leon lifted his leg and brought it down on the small coffee table, forcing Noah to release his bite as his head collided with the wood and smashed it.

Leon grabbed his leg, hobbling, looking down at the blood trickling from a large wound.

"You fucker!" Leon said, but was given no time to retaliate as Noah picked up the coffee table and slammed it into the kneecap of the same leg.

Leon fell, and Noah dragged himself across the floor, keeping hold of the coffee table, and struck it against Leon's kneecap once more, enjoying Leon's agitated shrieks.

Noah took a loose piece of wood from the table's remains and went to strike it against Leon's kneecap again, but Leon caught his hand, gripped his wrist, then threw a fist into Noah's jaw.

Noah did not let it throw him off and, as he lifted his head up, he bit the arm that gripped his wrist, forcing Leon to instinctively retract his hand.

This gave Noah another opportunity to slam the piece of wood into Leon's kneecap, forcing Leon to his back.

Noah turned to Leon's other knee, found the sharp, broken end of the piece of wood, and plunged it into his Leon's thigh, prompting another moan.

Noah backed up, panting, needing a moment's rest, and watched as Leon tried to take the piece of wood out of his thigh, only to find it to be too painful. He grimaced and, with a large, manly scream, he pulled it out and discarded it, leaving a few splinters sticking out of his skin.

Sensing an opportunity, Noah dove forward and punched the splinters, forcing them further into Leon's leg, and prompting another moan, each wail of pain from Leon another moment of vindication for Noah, another piece of revenge; a brief passage of satisfaction that he was providing the same amount of agony that Leon had forced on him.

Noah saw Leon wincing and took his chance, placing his hands together into one large fist, raising them high, and sending them soaring into Leon's face.

Noah crawled further along the floor, pushing himself on top of Leon, who tried to hit back, but Noah was able to block the punches.

He knew that he had to put Leon down permanently. Should Leon get out of this, he would regain his strength, and his rage would intensify, and Noah and his children's deaths would just be all the more painful.

He had no choice but to end this right now.

To end Leon.

And so he did something he thought he would never do.

He placed each thumb over Leon's eyes and pressed down, harder and harder.

Leon's hands fumbled at Noah, pushing his chin away, trying to grip his neck, unable to get anywhere near him.

But Leon was an experienced fighter, and the notion that

some privileged upper-middle-class man could beat someone who'd grown up fighting was ridiculous, and Leon punched the inside of Noah's elbows, thus causing his arms to capsize, preventing him from gauging Leon's eyes.

When Leon's eyes opened, they were bloodshot and full of insanity.

Noah did not stop.

He threw a fist, then another, then another. Leon formed a cage around his head with his arms, blocking every strike Noah threw, but Noah persisted.

He grabbed the loose bit of wood, pushed Leon's arms out of the way with one hand, and tried to stab his throat with sharp end, but Leon managed to get an arm free and punch Noah's chin.

By this point, Noah was quite used to pain, and it did not deter him. He swung the splintered side of the wood at Leon's throat, who nudged him off balance, forcing him to lodge a few splinters in Leon's shoulder instead.

Then Noah fought harder to control Leon's arms, pinning them behind his head, and placing the sharp end of the wood by Leon's throat.

This was it. It would be over with just one slit across the neck.

He took a breath then, just as he was about to end it, the front door opened.

"I wouldn't do that if I were you," Joanna said.

CHAPTER FIFTY-ONE

Noah's body went limp.

"Get the fuck off me," Leon grunted, and pushed Noah off.

Noah stared at Joanna, holding the dagger next to Mikey's throat.

Any hope that Mikey could have made it, that Mikey could have survived, could have found a way out… it was fool's hope.

Joanna had Mikey.

He was having to let Leon go.

And it was over.

Leon punched Noah in the face, hard, then again, releasing his anger at the audacity of Noah to muster even a small shred of self-defence.

"You fucking prick," Leon said, continuing to batter Noah. By the time he'd backed off, pushed himself onto the armchair and looked at the wounds on his leg, Noah's eye was black, his nose was skewed, and his right eye could barely open.

"Give me the boy," Leon demanded.

Joanna shoved Mikey at Leon. Mikey's nose was bloody. Why was it bloody?

"Give me the dagger."

She did as requested.

"No…" whimpered Noah.

"You brought this on yourself," Leon said.

Leon looked at Mikey, who looked back, his eyes wide.

He thought about the first time he saw those eyes. As Aubrey finished giving birth, on all fours, sweating and angry and in pain, and Noah wiped the perspiration from her brow as she lay down.

Then the doctor handed Mikey over.

Noah took Mikey in his arms, supporting his head as he'd seen other people do.

He'd have liked to have said his first feeling was of affection, but it wasn't, that came a few seconds later.

The first feeling was terror.

He was terrified he was going to screw it up. Not just as a dad, not just raising him, but in that moment, that he would drop Mikey, or not support his head properly, or not be able to change him.

Then came the love.

The overwhelming, world-ending love.

The need to protect, to keep safe from harm, and the vow that he always would. The belief that Mikey would encourage the love between him and Aubrey to grow even more. That he would be a father, the man of the house, in a home full of happiness.

There would be times he'd have to tell Mikey off, sure. He was ready for that. He had perfected his *go to your room* voice, and his *go sit on the naughty step* voice.

But he'd also perfected his *you are so special* voice, and his *I will love you forever* voice.

Those were the voices he thought of now, the ones he wanted to use as he looked into Mikey's eyes.

Mikey, the boy that took three years to conceive.

Mikey, the boy that showed him how to love without thought for himself, how to gain happiness from another's pleasure.

Mikey, the boy who was a miracle.

And Noah was forced to look into those eyes as Leon stabbed him, over and over, in the chest and in the neck, until Mikey didn't move anymore.

And those eyes no longer had the life he and Aubrey had given.

They just stared back at Noah with nothing behind them. No love, no hate, no fear and no happiness.

Just stared.

Just like the moment Mikey took his first breath, and the moment he took his last.

CHAPTER FIFTY-TWO

Noah looked to the floor.
He'd lost.
Not just the fight, not just the war – but everything.
He'd lost *everything.*

And he looked up at the one thing he had left to lose. Izzy. Lying so peacefully next to a corpse.

She was awake and wriggling. She was even smiling. Completely clueless about what was happening around her.

Were they going to kill her in front of him too?

And if they weren't, what were they going to do with her?

He couldn't bear thinking of it.

Leon forced himself to his feet, balancing on his one good leg, and used the furniture to take him to Joanna, who stood in the hallway.

He kissed her. Unashamedly passionate, right in front of Noah. On the lips, opening their mouths wide enough that Noah could see their tongues.

Then he picked up the cricket bat and turned to Noah.

Noah pushed himself to his knees. He may not want to die

on his knees, but he certainly did not want to die on his back. He at least wished to retain some dignity.

If he could.

After all, what had this evening been if not a process of humiliation? Taunting him, then battering him, then taking his family out one-by-one.

The Clarks had some fight back, though. Aubrey had managed to take out two of them. He was proud of her.

She did well at protecting her family.

Much better than he did.

And to think, they thought he'd care about an affair while his family's lives were on the line.

It didn't matter now. None of it did.

Nothing ever really mattered.

Just like this house. This stuff. This hallway and this living room that had been arranged symmetrically, perfectly positioned, was now a chaotic mess of furniture, with every previously unblemished surface coated in blood.

Leon hobbled to Noah's side. Placed the end of the cricket bat against the base of Noah's skull.

"Anything you want to say?"

"What could I possibly have to say to you?" Noah said through gritted teeth.

"Just thought you might like some final words."

"Go fuck yourself."

Leon grinned that same sick grin. "If you see my brother," he said, "then tell him he can rest easy now."

Noah went to open his mouth, but the strike of the cricket bat stopped him. His skull cracked, and he fell on his face.

He was still alive, but he wasn't moving. Just lying on his cheek, watching the blood spread across the floor, thinking of nothing but pain and the regret.

Leon lifted the bat above his head and brought it down on Noah's head again.

He felt his skull capsize in on his brain and he lost the ability to think or move.

So he just lay, still, absently staring, feeling the agony but thinking nothing about it.

The next strike knocked Noah unconscious, and his eyes closed.

Another strike, and another strike, and it was over.

Noah's life ended, and he ceased to exist.

There was no Heaven and no Hell. Instead, his body was reduced to absence. In a few years, no one would even remember he had been here.

CHAPTER FIFTY-THREE

A distant panting.

Talking, muffled, like it was underwater.

Blurred figures. Out of focus, but definite. The outlines hazy, but the presence unmistakable.

As Aubrey's eyes opened, ever so slightly, a marginal gap between her eyelids, she saw them.

Two fuzzy people. Man and woman. Sat together against the wall.

To them, it was over.

As it was for Noah. For Mikey.

And maybe Izzy…

Oh, God, Izzy...

Aubrey went to scream, to cry out, to call for her baby daughter, but no matter how much she pushed out her voice, only air came out.

There was a stinging sensation in her chest. She went to move her hand, to feel for the pain, to see if she could figure out what it was, but her hand slid.

Slid on what?

It was wet and thick.

She tried to move, but her body wasn't listening. Her mind urged her to get up, but her arms only twitched, and her fingers uncurled to reveal red on her palm and between the cracks of her digits.

Was she dead?

The woman moved closer to the man. Joanna. Leon. It was them. Their voices were hazy, but she recognised them.

From now until the end of time, she would be able to recognise those voices anywhere.

What had happened?

She tried to think. Tried to force her brain to work, to explore the depths of her absent memory.

She was stabbed.

Joanna.

Joanna stabbed her.

In the belly.

She bled. And now she had come around.

The pain was intense. She could barely move. Her eyes only flickered open and closed again.

But she was conscious, and she was aware enough to know that.

Joanna put her arm around Leon. Said something to him. It was only a few syllables long and raised in pitch in the middle of the sentence. Maybe it was *I love you* or something along those lines. In which case, it was sick. Four dead bodies, an injured woman, and a baby without a father were left in this house, and they could do nothing but express their love.

Izzy was crying.

Aubrey wasn't sure if Izzy had just started crying, or if she'd been crying for a while and she had only just tuned into it. It wasn't her loud wailing, but more like a constant murmur.

It didn't bother Leon nor Joanna, who sat with their backs to her, arms around each other, comforting each other.

Their backs were to her.

And she could feel for the door. Even if she didn't see it, even if it was not visible, she knew the direction in her own home.

So she reached out her right arm, wincing at the pain. The movement stretched the wound on her belly and it stung, but she kept going, pulling herself along the ground. To her, she was travelling great distance. In truth, she shifted an inch with each pull. It was going to take her a long time to get to the door.

And what then?

Would she crawl along the driveway like this? How far would she get before they noticed?

Perhaps the best thing she could do was play dead.

If it weren't for Izzy, she probably would have, but her maternal instincts raged against any other instinct she may have.

She *had* to get to her baby.

Yes, Izzy was crying, but that may just be in her head. She *had* to know Izzy was okay.

She pulled herself again, the carpet rubbing against her wound. Fortunately, she had grown quite numb, and whilst that burning would have felt like murder a few hours ago, now it just felt like the gentle heat of an open flame.

Inch by inch, she made it closer, past the cuddling lovers, and onto the tiles of the hallway.

She bypassed another body and reached her child.

Oh, how she wanted to take Izzy in her arms. Cradle her. Sing to her. Whisper nice words about the depths of her love.

As it was, dragging herself two or three metres had taken everything she had, and she could do nothing more than place a flopped hand on Izzy's chest.

Izzy's crying subsided, and Aubrey closed her eyes, feeling

her hand rising and lowering under the pressure of Izzy's tender breathing.

Feeling her daughter's lungs expand would be a great final moment, if that was what it was.

Then she heard a rustling outside. Steps on the gravel. The chaotic footfalls of Verity Cunningham, local Conservative MP.

And, amongst the confusion of her fading mind, she felt a glimmer of hope that salvation may be imminent.

CHAPTER FIFTY-FOUR

With her beige Burberry coat wrapped around her, Verity placed her silk scarf around her throat and left the house, locking it as she did.

It was late. At least, it was late enough. Soon it would be morning, and the time for darkness covering dark deeds would be over.

She shuffled to the end of her driveway, passing the roses planted by her gardener yesterday afternoon. They were all skewwhiff, pointing in the wrong directions, and she remembered telling Rosemary that she was meant to plant them all so they faced in the exact same direction – toward the house. A simple request, one that was not followed, and depending on how her mood took her that morning – which would be dependent on the next few hours – that girl may find herself applying for universal credit before the week was out.

"Stupid girl," she muttered, stepping past the rose bush that over hung the driveway's edge, and the grass that had gone a whole week without being cut.

Whatever was she paying that dastardly girl for?

Once she reached the end of her driveway, she turned onto

the pavement and approached the Clark's driveway. She used the spare key they'd given her in case of emergencies to let herself through the gate, and scoffed at their garden. In fairness to Rosemary, at least she didn't create this haphazard mess. She assumed Noah had done this gardening himself, or maybe Aubrey, or heck, maybe they let Mikey do it. It was a blot on the image of this neighbourhood and she had always disliked this family for it.

She charged down the driveway, staring through the living room as she did. It was dark. No movement.

There were only so many times she could come around to talk about a lasagne – which, frankly, was disgusting. She'd lied about its taste, her chef made awful lasagnes, but it was the item of food she made the quickest so it would have to do. What's more, it was going to seem most irregular if she were to ask for her lasagne dish back at almost 5.00 a.m. Then again, she'd be surprised if Noah or Aubrey answered the door.

She rang the doorbell and stepped back. Admired the moon and the stars. It was a clear night. She'd always wanted to frolic in the subject of astronomy, but never had the time. Perhaps it could be a retirement project. Then again, it might require too much effort on her part.

No one answered, and Verity did not wish to ring again. *Ah, to heck with it,* she figured, and she opened the door.

There, in the middle of the floor, was Declan's body. Next to Izzy. Next to Aubrey, with her hand on the baby's chest, and a large trail of blood behind her.

She placed her hands over her mouth and gasped.

Leon and Joanna rushed out of the living room and came to a halt as they saw her. They stayed like this for a moment, staring at her, in a stand-off, neither knowing what to do.

That was, until Verity marched forward and took the knife from Leon's belt.

"What an imbecile," she stated. "Can't you see she's still alive?" She knelt beside Aubrey. "Once again, I have to do this for you."

Verity stuck a knife into Aubrey's gut, twisted it, and withdrew the knife again.

"And now my prints are on the knife," she said, placing the knife in Leon's hands and using his t-shirt to wipe the blood off her hands.

"Well you made a bloody mess of it, didn't you?" she said. "Almost letting a survivor go."

Leon bowed his head.

"Sorry, Aunt Verity," he said.

CHAPTER FIFTY-FIVE

"There's only so many times I can come around to talk about a lasagne dish, you know."

Leon felt embarrassed in front of Joanna. He could feel her stare, the grin, the sniggers. He could tell she was finding it funny that Aunt Verity could just march in here after they'd done all the work and make him feel ashamed.

"Let's see what other mess you've left."

Verity marched past Leon, into the living room, and looked back and forth with her hands on her hips, surveying Noah and Mikey's dead bodies. She stepped through to the dining room, where Roman's body remained, and returned to the hallway.

She stood in front of Leon, hands on hips, tongue in cheek, and went to say something. Unable to find the words, she slapped him instead, hard, across the cheek.

"Do you want to explain this to me?"

"Explain what, Aunt Verity?"

She slapped him again.

Joanna laughed.

Verity looked over her shoulder at Joanna.

"Excuse me?" Verity said.

Joanna lifted her hands up as if to surrender, but the cheeky smirk was all Verity saw.

"Do you have a problem?" Verity asked.

"Hey, you're not my aunt."

"No, but I am the one who's going to have to deal with the repercussions of this, you little shit. You think it looks good for this to happen in my constituency? It's thanks to me you were even able to make it this far."

Joanna sniggered again.

Leon's body stiffened. Joanna didn't know his aunt, didn't know what she could do.

"Babe, please don't," Leon urged her.

"I just think it's funny," Joanna continued.

"Whatever is so funny, you little hussy?" Verity demanded.

"Like, you hated his mum. You didn't give a shit when you married into money. You didn't speak to her, even when she was dying. And what, now you have her son acting like he's your little minion?"

"You don't know a thing."

"I know that a rich bitch like you doesn't want to get your hands dirty, so you have your nephew do all your dirty work for you."

Verity took the knife back from Leon's hands, charged toward Joanna and, before Joanna could fully raise her hands to block herself, Verity swung the knife into Joanna's throat, held it there, then pulled it out again.

Joanna fell to her knees, desperately pressing her hands against the wound, blood squirting from between her fingers, ruining the wallpaper.

Verity stood aside to ensure she didn't get hit by the stream of red, then swung the knife again, landing it into the other side of Joanna's throat.

Joanna fell to her back, staring at the ceiling, her body

convulsing, her arms scrambling. Verity stood over her, watching. Waiting. Once Joanna had stopped moving, she shoved the knife back into Leon's hands and scowled at him, forcing him to drop his head in shame once more.

"This is your fault!" she snapped.

Leon looked at his girlfriend and refused to cry. He wanted to well-up. He'd really loved her. But he knew Verity would not have it.

As it was, Aunt Verity was pacing back and forth, one hand on her lip, deep in thought.

"You've made a pig's ear of this, you really have…"

Leon bowed his head further, but kept an eye on Joanna's corpse, hoping she would wake up, open her eyes, that she had somehow survived.

But she hadn't. There was no chance she'd have survived that.

"You let your brother be killed, your accomplice, and then your girlfriend… The impudence… She knew her place, did she not?"

"I don't know, Aunt Verity."

"What do you mean, you don't know? In my day, a girl would never dare speak to her elders like that! It's disgusting."

She stared at the knife held loosely in Leon's hands.

"And now my DNA will be all over that weapon."

Leon looked at Joanna again.

"Oh, for Christ's sake, what is it?"

"Nothing, Aunt Verity, I just… I really loved her."

"Oh shut up, you little faggot. You didn't love her. She just happened to be more attractive than the girls you went to school with. There are plenty more like her. And what on earth is wrong with your leg?"

She scowled at the bloody wounds on his leg.

"Really, Leon, I don't quite believe the mess you've made."

She turned toward the door and huffed.

"We need to get rid of that weapon, or it's going to tie me to this. Drive me to the bridge, and let's be done with it. I don't want anything in my car, so… let's take yours."

She looked repulsed as she said it.

She walked toward the door.

"What about the baby?" Leon asked, indicating the child who was still wriggling next to its mother.

"What about it?" Verity asked.

Leon paused, went to object, then thought better of it.

"Nothing, Aunt Verity," he said, and followed her to his car.

They would go to the river and dump the knife, then he would return her to her home, and her part in all of this would be done.

At least, it seemed that simple when they left the house.

CHAPTER FIFTY-SIX

Verity sat in the back and dropped her head below the window. The last thing she needed was for a constituent to recognise her. She could just imagine the headline.

Tory MP in Cahoots With Local Ruffian.

She had an image to maintain, and she was starting to regret ever being involved in this. But that was her nephew for you – if she ever wanted him to succeed in something, he would need her intervention.

She wanted Jamal's death to be avenged.

She wanted those lawyers to suffer.

But she couldn't do this herself, nor could she find real justice through politics. This was the only way.

And she had felt like a fool having to continually return to the home to check on the status of the task under the pretence of a pathetic little lasagne that, let's be fair, tasted like the underside of a train seat.

"You okay, Aunt Verity?"

"What?"

"I said, you okay?"

"What do you mean, 'you okay?' The question is 'are you okay?' What, are you too good to have to muster another syllable?"

"Are you okay, Aunt Verity?"

"Yes, I'm fine. Just focus on driving and try not to mess that up too."

They passed a cyclist on his way to work. She sunk lower, lifting the collars on her coat up and holding a hand over her face. The foggy early morning light was starting to create clarity through the darkness, and the possibility of being recognised was getting stronger.

Oh, why did she have to come along to dispose of the weapon anyway?

Oh, yes, that's right – because she couldn't even trust her stupid nephew to chuck a knife into a river correctly.

He was too like his mother.

He turned a corner sharply, which threw her against the window, and she was about to scald him when a wailing interrupted her.

She looked behind them.

A police car. Sirens on.

Speeding up. Coming closer.

Leon began to speed the car up.

"Oh, just let them pass, would you?"

Then she realised – Leon wasn't going to let them pass. They were coming for him.

But why? Surely no neighbours saw them.

Then she realised, and she shook her head whilst rolling her eyes.

"Leon…"

"Yes, Aunt Verity?"

"Is this a stolen car?"

"…It might be."

Her fists curled and she struck out at the back of the car seat.

"What the bloody hell is wrong with you!"

"Does it matter?"

She glanced over her shoulder at the police car chasing them.

"Pull over," she instructed.

"But–"

"I said pull the damn car over."

"Are you sure, Aunt Verity?"

"Did I stutter?"

Leon reluctantly slowed the car down and stopped at the side of the road.

The police car stopped behind them, but no one stepped out yet. They were most likely discussing how to proceed.

"What should I do now, Aunt Verity?"

She looked at his eyes in the rear-view mirror.

She almost said to him, *you are to do nothing.*

But she didn't.

Because of what she was about to do.

The police officer stepped out of his car. Approached them.

As soon as he was in ear shot, Verity screamed. Loud. Hard. Frantic. Like she was being mugged or attacked or raped at that very moment.

"Aunt Verity?" Leon asked, confused.

She ignored him and banged on the window as the officer came into view.

"Help!" she shouted. "Help, please! Help! Help me!"

"Aunt Verity?"

"Get out the car!" the officer instructed Leon. He'd taken a baton from his belt. "Get out the car now!"

The officer turned to his radio and requested backup, and the other officer came out of the car.

Verity did not stop screaming. She bashed the window, appearing distraught, out of control, as hysterical as a woman in distress could possibly be.

And they bought it. Of course they would. She was an MP. She was rich. She was too old and too fragile and too feminine to be able to fight a young man. The only explanation was that she was kidnapped.

Leon looked at her in the rear-view mirror again. Frowning. Confused.

She didn't react to him. She continued to scream and shout and batter the window and beg for release, oh please release me, please save me, my deranged nephew came in the night and took me from my home, please, oh please…

The officer smashed the window with his baton, evidently tired of waiting.

Leon didn't hesitate. He shoved the door open, knocking it into the officer's groin, and ran, the officer giving chase.

The other officer appeared at Verity's side straight away, asking if she was okay.

"Oh, thank you, thank you!" she said, wrapping her arms around his neck, thanking him incessantly, so pleased that the brave man could come and rescue the dainty little woman, and hoping that they caught the scoundrel who did this.

They called an ambulance and made sure she was all right while they waited to hear whether the other officer caught Leon.

CHAPTER FIFTY-SEVEN

The early morning sun made Leon squint.

It had been a long night, one that had worn him down both physically and mentally, and he could feel himself lagging. His wounded calf stung harder with every step, and his legs felt like they were wading through water.

The police officer was almost at his back.

Leon was going nowhere now. There was nothing but fields before him, and he had no doubt the officer had called for more officers, and there would be more fairly soon.

He was done.

So he stopped. Turned around. Put his hands in the air.

The police officer slowed down to a walking pace and took the last few steps toward Leon slowly.

The sun illuminated this officer's face and, as his features became clearer, Leon had a vague sense of recognition. He was sure he knew this officer. Then again, he'd met a lot of piggies. They hardly left him alone, even when he wasn't breaking the law. He was bound to come across the same one every now and then.

Except, he really recognised this man.

The man approached, a wide grin from cheek to cheek.

Leon squinted to see the man's face up close.

No...

It couldn't be possible...

His hair was longer. He had a beard now. His was stockier. But behind it all, those eyes were exactly the same...

"You," Leon said

"Me?" PC Levi Isaacs said. "No, this is about you."

"I thought I got one of my boys to–"

"They barely put a bruise on me."

Leon was shaking. Fatigue mixed with rage. He almost cried his anger was so strong. This man... He'd killed Leon's brother...

Leon went to throw a fist, but his arm was loose and tired and he'd barely swung it before a big, beefy fist landed in his mouth, knocking him to the ground.

He spat blood and, along with that, a tooth.

The fucker...

Leon went to stand again, but Levi swung his fist into the side of Leon's head and knocked him back down.

Even against a man this big, and with a punch like this, Leon would normally stand a chance. He may not be as big, but he was wily, and quick, and slick.

But he was also exhausted.

His leg was throbbing, and he tried to push himself up onto his good leg.

Evidently seeing that Leon's calf was in a poor condition, Isaacs stomped on it with the heel of his boot, causing a large scream to echo into the distance.

But there was no one around to hear it.

No witnesses.

This man could kill him, and no one could say it wasn't justified, as there was no one else around to see. Even if it went to trial, which it probably wouldn't, it would be the same outcome, and he would get away with it again.

And in that way, Leon knew he wasn't going to win. He knew there was no use in fighting.

He put his hands up in surrender. He would have his vengeance, but for now, he had to live to see another day.

Levi, however, couldn't give two shits about Leon's raised hands. He swung another fat fist into Leon's cheek.

Leon tried to push himself to his feet as he muttered, "What are you doing? I'm giving up. You got me."

Isaacs threw another fist into Leon's head, knocking him face first into the mud. He lifted his head, groggy, filthy.

Levi stomped on his head and everything went fuzzy. The field, the sky, the boot, it all became distant background noise, and Leon hated himself for being beaten this way.

Levi went to his knees, lifted his baton high into the air, and looked his victim in the eyes.

"You won't get away with this," Leon said, lying, just hoping that his begging would make him stop.

Levi laughed. Of course he would. He was one-on-one with a dangerous criminal, of course his self-defence would be justified!

Would anyone even argue, considering who the victim was?

"Please…" Leon begged. "Please, I beg you… Don't…"

Levi brought the baton down upon Leon's head. Blood splattered over the grass and over Levi's uniform.

Leon's body went limp.

Looks like the fucker received his comeuppance after all.

CHAPTER FIFTY-EIGHT

Verity was inconsolable. A wreck. Unable to control her hysteria. It took a lot of effort for the officer to calm her down with his look of reassurance, and his hand on her back whilst repeating that it would be okay.

"You're the local MP, aren't you?" he asked.

"Y-y-yes, I am…"

"My name is PC Carl Briggs – please call me Carl. And you say he's your nephew?"

"He – he – he was angry that I s-s-stopped talking to his mother… She died recently…"

"Oh, I am sorry to hear that."

His radio buzzed and he excused himself for a moment, stepping away.

Verity sighed. This was an exhausting performance, and she was growing tired. It had been a long night.

When he finished talking on the radio, he paused for a moment, seemingly gathering his thoughts. She took this opportunity to renew her tears, and was sobbing again by the time he came back over to her.

"He got him," the officer said.

"Yeah?"

Verity panicked. She hadn't thought about what would happen if they caught him… He would have his story to tell, and it would contradict hers. Yes, hers would probably be believed over his, but it still wasn't worth the risk. Did she have any contacts in prison she could use to silence him?

But, as it turned out, she wouldn't need to.

"They were in a fight," the officer added. "I'm sorry to have to tell you this, but, well – the boy's dead."

"He's – what?"

Wow.

Well…

Huh.

This was an unforeseen event.

She was upset, of course, as it was her nephew, but it certainly did solve things.

Sirens blared in the distance, quickly growing closer, and more police cars pulled up. Carl directed them to the field, and they ran to the crime scene as he stayed with the hysterical woman who was unable to control her emotions.

Carl collected some tissue from the car and handed it to her.

"Thank you," she said, her voice faint and weak, and dabbed her eyes.

"Your nephew was prime suspect in a home invasion from a few days ago," Carl informed her. "You may have seen it on the news. A lawyer called Michael Logan and his family was murdered. He–"

Carl's radio blared once again.

"Excuse me," he said, and stepped away.

Verity tried to hear what he was saying, but she only caught snippets. Words like *murder* and *another one*. When he returned a minute later, he had a solemn look.

"He's been involved in another home invasion tonight," Carl said.

"Oh no, with whom?"

"Noah Clark."

"Oh my, he's my neighbour. Do you think he did it before he abducted me?"

"It's quite possible. Perhaps he wished to use you as leverage for his escape."

"Oh how awful. Is Noah and his family okay?"

"Unfortunately not. Leon's accomplices don't appear to have survived, and two of the family are dead."

"Oh dear."

She put on her *oh how awful* face and looked down.

So far, this was going swimmingly. The gullible fool was believing every word, and he–

Wait. Hang on.

Did he say *two* survived?

"Who are the deceased?" she asked.

"Noah Clark and his son, Michael."

"And… the survivors?"

"The baby survived, and his wife is in intensive care."

"His wife?"

"Aubrey Clark."

"Is she going to be okay?"

"I don't know."

"Could you find out?"

He hesitated, then said, "I really shouldn't."

"Please, I'm concerned."

With a huff, he turned to his radio. "Can we get an update on the status of Aubrey Clark?"

They waited, every second feeling like an hour, every moment a dreaded moment of doom.

This woman could ruin everything.

How had she survived? She'd had a knife wound to the chest and a knife wound to the gut…

Dammit. Verity should have gone for the neck.

How foolish of her.

"She's just out of ICU," the person on the radio said. "They believe she's going to live. They are going to try bringing her round soon."

"She's fine," Carl clarified. "She's alive."

Verity forced a smile. It was the toughest smile she'd ever had to produce, but she forced it anyway.

Perhaps Aubrey didn't remember.

Perhaps she'd never remember.

Or, perhaps, she would wake up one day and it would all come hurtling back to her.

Verity couldn't take the risk.

"Could I go see her?" she asked.

"I'm not sure…"

"Please. As the local MP, I feel it's my duty to be there. To ensure she's okay. It's my responsibility, please, just – take me."

He paused. Watched her.

"You need to come to the station first," he said. "Then someone will take you."

"Oh, bless you. You are such a kind man."

CHAPTER FIFTY-NINE

Verity sat through a few hours of procedure at the station, her foot tapping the floor, trying not to show her impatience.

Aubrey had seen her.

Aubrey was conscious when Verity dug that knife into her.

It was a loose end she could not deal with.

Finally, after what seemed like far too long, Carl took her to the hospital. When they arrived at the building, reporters were already waiting outside. Verity wondered how the media had arrived so quickly, then decided she could use it to her advantage.

"You," she said, pointing at the nearest photographer; a young man with pimples and wide, innocent eyes. "Follow me."

He did as he was told, and Carl led them through the sterile corridors of the hospital. The walls were cream and the floor was tiled. Everything was plain, except for the odd poster about smoking or recognising diabetes, and frequent hand sanitising stations. It was a huge building, and if she were on her own, it would have taken Verity a long time to track Aubrey down. As it was, Carl seemed to have good knowledge of the layout, and was able to lead her.

Aubrey wasn't in a cubicle like the rest of the patients. She was in a room, with windows shielded by curtains, and a hospital security standing outside the door. Carl opened the door for her.

"Please, could you give us a moment," she requested.

"I really shouldn't. She's a witness to an investigation."

"I know." Verity put a hand on his chest and smiled sweetly. She was just an old lady, what damage could she do? "I just think she needs a friend. A happy neighbour."

Carl thought about this. "I'll wait here," he said.

Verity smiled at him, told the photographer to wait by the window, and entered.

The door shut and Aubrey looked up.

She was weak. Bruised. Attached to a machine that beeped rhythmically. As soon as she saw Verity her eyes widened, and the beeping quickened pace. She looked around for help, but they were hidden from view, the curtains concealed their interaction.

"Please," Verity said. "If I was going to kill you, it would already have been arranged."

Aubrey's eyes widened as Verity approached her. But all Verity did when she reached Aubrey's side was puff her pillows and pull the duvet further up.

"Are they making you comfortable?" she asked.

Aubrey, still staring, gave a tiny nod.

"Wonderful. You know, I am a member of parliament, so I do have some pull, and if there's anything that can make your stay here more comfortable, I'd be happy to have it arranged."

Still staring, she gave a small shake of the head.

"Well, you let me know if you change your mind. I just want you to be aware of the power that I have. I can make your life so much more pleasant." She leant in, close enough that Aubrey could feel the warmth of her stale breath. "And, likewise, I can make it unpleasant too."

Verity lifted the duvet up at the side and surveyed the wounds on Aubrey's belly. They were covered in bandages, but a little dot of blood still seeped through.

"Oh, dear," Verity said. "Those are quite the injuries, aren't they?"

Aubrey tried opening her mouth, but she was too weak.

"Go on, you can do it."

Aubrey managed to form the words, and forced out a faint whisper. "What do you want from me?"

Verity grinned. "That is the correct question."

Verity stepped away from her. Turned around. Sighed. Collected herself. Considered her words. Then turned back.

"Your husband left a will, yes?"

Aubrey didn't answer.

"I would appreciate an answer, Aubrey."

Aubrey nodded.

"He was the sole earner in the family, wasn't he? Meaning that you would struggle to support yourself and your baby without his will. Correct?"

Aubrey nodded.

"And Noah had life insurance as well?"

Aubrey nodded.

"Wonderful. And I assume you would like that money?"

Aubrey nodded.

"Well, if you say a single word to anyone about my involvement, then you will be accused of involvement yourself. You will be investigated. And they will find compelling evidence that you were complicit with your home invaders."

Verity stepped toward Aubrey, her short stature managing to tower over her, and said in a low, husky voice, "Trust me, they will find something."

Verity ran a hand over Aubrey's hair, straightening it.

"If you are accused of murder and, of course, subsequently convicted for your involvement in this crime, you will receive no money, and Izzy will go into foster care. You do understand that, don't you?"

Aubrey's eyes narrowed into a glare.

"Clarification, please, Aubrey."

Aubrey reluctantly nodded.

"Wonderful. And, don't forget, you were an adulterous wife. You betrayed the man you murdered. You have motive. There is an image I could easily create about you. As annoying as the media can be, it is quite easy to make them my ally."

Verity's grin widened.

"It's about power, you see, Aubrey, which is determined by what you have. You had more than Leon and his friends, so you had the power. I, however, have much, much more than you do. Which means that *I* have the power, Aubrey. I have it all."

Verity stepped to the window and pulled one of the curtains apart. The photographer, excited at the opportunity to get the perfect shot of the victim, quickly aimed his lens.

"Now," Verity said, stepping beside Aubrey and grinning for the camera, "smile if you understand."

Aubrey forced a smile.

Together, their picture was taken.

After a few flashes, Verity drew the curtains back again.

She stepped toward the door, paused, and turned toward Aubrey, gaining satisfaction at her pain.

"Thank you, Aubrey," she said. "You have made what could have been a very difficult, painful conversation, into a wonderful moment where we truly seem to understand each other."

Verity went to leave, but was halted by Aubrey's voice.

"And what about when I have the power?"

Verity turned back toward Aubrey. "Excuse me?"

"What about the day when I have the status? Maybe I'll run for parliament."

"Please, unless you win the lottery I think I will be okay. Just think of your baby growing up with an incarcerated mother if you need motivation – that should be enough for you."

Verity went to leave, but was halted once more.

"You never gave a shit about Jamal or Leon, did you?"

"Excuse me?"

"Was this all for revenge – or was it just because you can?"

Verity chuckled. "My dear, everything anyone ever does is just because they can."

Verity opened the door and left, escorted by Carl.

Aubrey remained alone. In the bed. Desperate to see Izzy, needing to know she was okay.

Knowing that she would remain silent until the day she died.

Verity was right.

Unfortunately.

Verity was many things – a liar, a cheat, a corrupt piece of shit – but she was also correct.

Only the powerful could be corrupted.

Only those with more to lose can be made desperate not to lose it.

The world wasn't set up to favour a widowed single mother. It was set up for rich politicians.

But someday.

Someday…

Aubrey would have status. Would have a great job. Great power.

She would claw her way even further up the class system until it was her that had more to cling onto than Verity Cunningham.

And when that day came, she would bury Verity with all

the other skeletons she'd have to discard on her way up the ladder.

She would reach it.

She would. She knew it. She believed it.

As impossible as such a dream might be.

JOIN RICK WOOD'S READER'S GROUP...

And get **Roses Are Red So Is Your Blood** for free!

Join at **www.rickwoodwriter.com/sign-up**

AVAILABLE IN THE BLOOD SPLATTER
BOOKS SERIES...

Psycho B*tches
Shutter House
This Book is Full of Bodies
Haunted House
Home Invasion
Woman Scorned

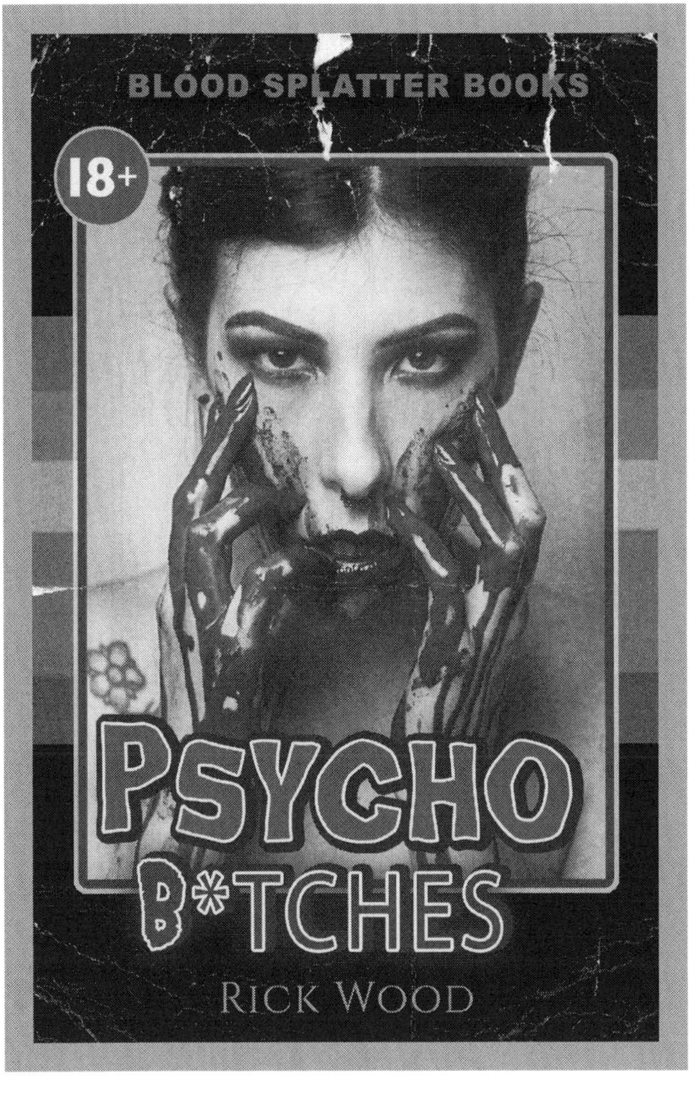
BLOOD SPLATTER BOOKS
18+
PSYCHO
B*TCHES
RICK WOOD

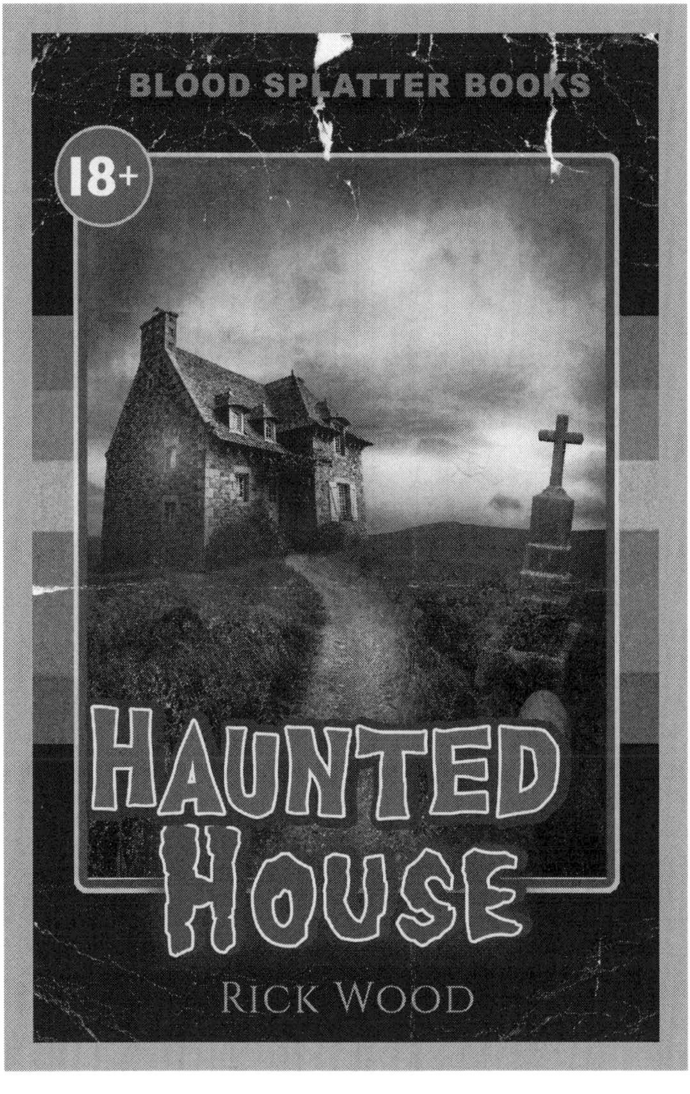
BLOOD SPLATTER BOOKS
18+
HAUNTED HOUSE
RICK WOOD

BLOOD SPLATTER BOOKS

18+

This Book Is Full of BODIES

RICK WOOD

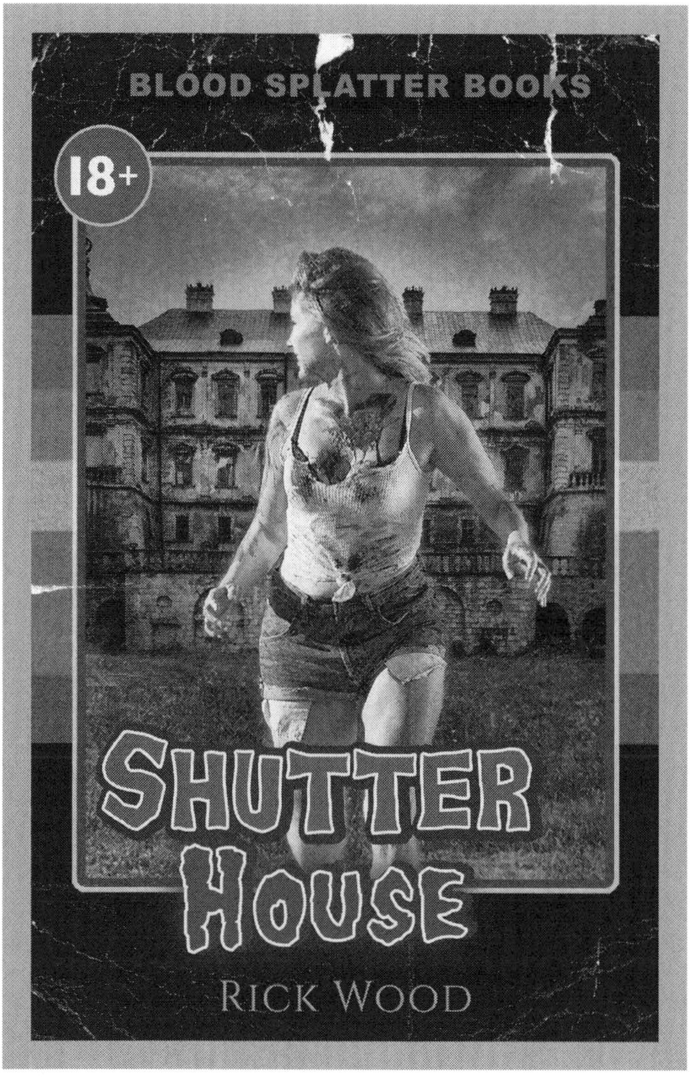
BLOOD SPLATTER BOOKS
18+
SHUTTER
HOUSE
RICK WOOD

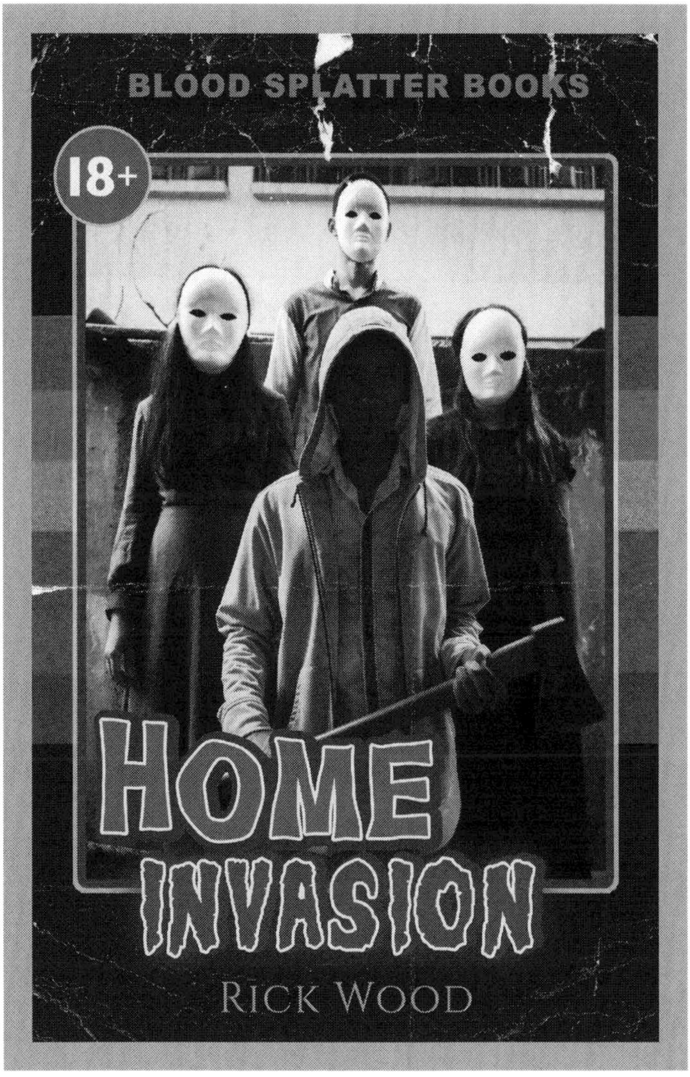
BLOOD SPLATTER BOOKS
18+
HOME
INVASION
RICK WOOD

BLOOD SPLATTER BOOKS

18+

WOMAN
SCORNED

RICK WOOD

ALSO BY RICK WOOD…

BOOK ONE IN THE SENSITIVES SERIES

THE SENSITIVES

RICK WOOD

RICK
WOOD

CIA
ROSE
BOOK
ONE

AFTER
THE DEVIL
HAS WON